"A STUNNING ACHIEVEMENT . . . not limited to the gay experience, but touches upon the very nature of the human condition . . . renews faith in the American novel. . . . One of the finest (and certainly most moving) novels of the year."
—James Fritzhand, in *The Advocate*

"ELOQUENT, IMPASSIONED . . . centers on a homosexual son's conflict with his father, yet whirls into every corner of a family's grief, desperation and love . . . a literary accomplishment on the order of Christina Stead's *The Man Who Loved Children*." —Eliot Fremont-Smith in *Diversion*

"Reads almost like an old romance, full of family tales, beckoning dreams . . . brilliant, distinguished, powerful, seductively readable."
—*Publishers Weekly*

"SENSITIVE AND ORIGINAL . . . beautifully sustained and often disturbing . . . at once deeply personal and universal." —*New York Native*

ROBERT FERRO, who lives in Manhattan with the "Nick" of his novel, has traveled extensively in Europe and the Caribbean. He attended the Iowa Writer's Workshop in the 1960s, and is the author of *The Others*.

THE FAMILY of MAX DESIR

Robert Ferro

A PLUME BOOK

NEW AMERICAN LIBRARY

NEW YORK AND SCARBOROUGH, ONTARIO

PUBLISHER'S NOTE

This novel is a work of fiction. Names, characters, places, and incidents are either the product of the author's imagination or are used fictitiously, and any resemblance to actual persons, living or dead, events, or locales is entirely coincidental.

This is an authorized reprint of a hardcover edition published by E. P. Dutton, Inc.
The hardcover edition was published simultaneously in Canada by Clarke, Irwin & Company Limited, Toronto and Vancouver.

Designed by Earl Tidwell

Ⓟ PLUME TRADEMARK REG. U.S. PAT. OFF. AND FOREIGN COUNTRIES REGISTERED TRADEMARK—MARCA REGISTRADA HECHO EN WESTFORD, MASS., U.S.A.

SIGNET, SIGNET CLASSIC, MENTOR, PLUME, MERIDIAN and NAL BOOKS are published *in the United States* by New American Library, 1633 Broadway, New York, New York, 10019, *in Canada* by The New American Library of Canada Limited, 81 Mack Avenue, Scarborough, Ontario M1L 1M8

LIBRARY OF CONGRESS CATALOGING IN PUBLICATION DATA
Ferro, Robert.
    The family of Max Desir.
    I. Title.
PS3556.E76F3   1984   813'.54   84-4906
ISBN 0-452-25587-2

First Plume Printing, September, 1984

1 2 3 4 5 6 7 8 9

PRINTED IN THE UNITED STATES OF AMERICA

FOR MICHAEL GRUMLEY

THEN CAME A LONG GENTLE CURVE IN THE HIGHWAY, LIKE THE bottom of an arabic letter. On the outside of the curve lay a flat sloping field and the remnants of an orchard. It was a hot day at the end of August, 1977. The man at the wheel of the car was Dan Defilippo, Max Desir's uncle. He was driving to Philadelphia to see a man to whom he hoped to sell printing supplies. On the seat next to him a heavy machine of some printing use shifted as the car entered the curve. Traffic was light. A car of coeds returning to Temple University followed fifty yards behind. As the machine leaned toward him, Dan put out his arm to steady it. This sudden movement did not startle or alarm him particularly; nor was it the first time it had shifted. But as he steadied it on the seat he felt a tingling sensation rise up his left arm and shoulder, so that he had difficulty gripping the wheel. He had the impression of being hit with something soft and wet, like thrown fruit. It seemed to splatter behind his eyes. The car left the highway, cas-

1

ually it appeared, and drew a gentle curve of its own across the field, although on the slope it picked up speed. An impact, to which last purpose a certain ancient apple tree had survived, threw him thirty feet clear.

The coeds were student nurses at the university hospital nearby. Still, for five or six minutes he did not breathe, and in that time most of his brain died.

In intensive care they said the brain stem was damaged; that cranial fluid, which had built up to cause severe pressure, must be drained. His face and body were covered with plum-dark bruises in swirls like marbleized paper, but he was otherwise unharmed. He lay amidst the chaotic medical welter of emergency. A respirator tube entered directly into his trachea. Others were fitted into his nose and the vein in his wrist. His head was tilted back awkwardly, to accommodate the tubes, but to Max this angle seemed more the result of the struggle Dan's spirit was waging, in a place just behind the eyelids—a war in which the spirit fought for space in which to continue living.

The days went by. The bruises lightened, faded. The family was allowed, two at a time, to spend five minutes of each hour at Dan's bedside. They were encouraged by the nurses to talk to him, to call him back, as if he were just off in the distance, headed in the wrong direction. Max could not bring himself to say a word. He held his hand instead, and thought thoughts that beckoned, that reached into a void of sleep and oblivion. The nurses told of patients emerging from comas remembering everything that had been said to them. They had heard and understood but were unable to respond.

The women wore dark clothes to the hospital. It was an endless wake. Their strengths, their reserves were drained. Anxiety, fear, strain, fatigue, one by one were drawn in Marie Desir's eyes, as if these emotions could help in some prescription for her brother's recovery. Dan's wife, Phoebe, seemed sturdier. She cried often quietly for short periods, after which she seemed restored. There were dark circles under her eyes and she didn't look well, but her skin did not begin to whiten, sag and crease up like Marie's; the capillaries did not suddenly map themselves out on her cheeks. Phoebe was younger, stronger, with a history of self-reliance. She saw perhaps what a distance lay ahead of them. It was Marie who seemed to have made the decision to decline as Dan declined, to release her grip on life until he regained his.

After three weeks intensive care was no longer thought necessary. Dan had stabilized into a deep, apparently irreversible coma. Sometimes his eyes opened. The pupils reacted to light, to movement, like those of a small, wary animal in the hollow of a tree. At times he would yawn, stretching his mouth around an endless moment of air. His younger brother Frank spent hours of every day speaking to him, convinced he could eventually get through. It did not seem to Frank that any amount of blackened brain could prevent him from calling his brother back.

Toward the end of the second month Dan made a struggle and lost. It was as if he tried to wake, to fight his way back. Alternate periods of rigidity and relaxation progressed through a feverish restlessness that built nearly to convulsions. Finally his eyes opened and swept the room, resting momentarily on everyone present. The eyes blinked once; round, focused and clear. Then they closed. The mind, as if having come to the surface for a moment, sank down; the fever cooled. The body lay abandoned and derelict, anchored by tubes. In another month he was moved, to a nursing home near Phoebe on Long Island. He was given fourteen hundred calories of nutrients a day, intravenously. His face seemed younger, without lines or strain. A therapist exercised his useless arms and legs twice a day. Marie and John Desir went to see him regularly, usually on Sunday. Max asked his aunt Phoebe if she understood that he did not want to see Dan out there. And Phoebe replied that they must all deal with this in their own way.

I

MAX'S MOTHER, MARIE DESIR, BORN DEFILIPPO—SIXTY-EIGHT
years old, five foot two, favoring Barbara Stanwyck playing a lady—was shopping for another dark dress in a mall
not far from her home. She was to meet her maid Greta
for lunch in fifteen minutes and was in something of a
hurry. A glamorous young woman carrying a tray of perfume came up beside her.

Would you like to try our newest scent? the woman
asked, spritzing a tiny flaçon in Mrs Desir's direction. A
nauseating moment of sweet flowers and lacquer went by.

It's called Lovewish. The woman smiled, waiting for
a compliment.

It's horrible. Marie Desir waved the air in front of
her face. You shouldn't do that to people, she said, and
left the store.

She had always shopped: even before her husband's
pleasant business success shopping had been a focus of
her life, an activity she enjoyed and even needed as an

expression of hope, satisfaction, anxiety. Once, during an earlier period, when her four children were young, a man came to the back door and said he had been sent to check the water softener in the basement. She let him in and he went down the stairs. A moment later he called up to her.

Hey, lady, come down here. I want to show you something.

She was alone, in her nightgown and robe. Just a minute, she replied, and shut the cellar door. Taking her pocketbook and keys she left the house, dressed as she was, and drove to a department store. There she bought her way out of her fright, starting with underclothes and nylons, shoes, gloves, a dress and a hat to replace the nightclothes. For the next few hours she bought everything she liked, everything she needed—two thousand dollars' worth—a fortune that reflected her perception of the dangerous man in the basement.

Greta, the maid, had been hired as part of the new regime, now in its tenth year, when the Desirs moved into a big house they had built near their married children, Jack, Robin and Penny. Greta Hollis was a tall, sturdy Dutch woman in her mid-fifties. When Max happened to see Garbo out walking on Fifth Avenue, his first thought was of how much she had come to resemble his mother's maid. And the next time he was home he had Greta put on a pair of dark glasses and Marie's fur coat, and made her stand in front of a mirror. I'm telling you, Greta, Max said, you look just like her.

The house was the size of a small country club, tall and white, with six two-story columns across the front, fifteen rooms, a twenty-five-foot high den, billiard room, sauna, many unused bedrooms and, as Marie put it, the kitchen of life. To her it was like a house in a Bette Davis movie—Charlotte Vale's house, Mrs Skeffington's house

—with generous spaces and details, pilasters and cakelike moldings, with deep fireplaces, a winding staircase and niches filled with dogwood.

Aside from the fact of her employment, Greta's attachment to Marie was more like that of a big, adopted daughter. Marie had always had cleaning help but never a full-time maid. And Greta, who was hired as a necessity, had therefore been incorporated into the family. She worked hard and kept the place pristine, but beyond anything else she was a companion, and she and Marie spent a great deal of time together. Today they were to meet at a restaurant called Hannigan's, a recent discovery, a glass conservatory near the shopping center with jungle plants and intricate luncheon plates for ladies and their friends, or daughters, or maids.

The hostess was busy elsewhere when Greta arrived and she had trouble locating Mrs Desir. Then she saw her, sitting alone at a table framed in a high window at the side, and she rushed over because Mrs Desir had her face in her hands and was sitting quite still, apparently crying. Greta put her hand on Mrs Desir's shoulder and said, What's the matter? What's wrong?

Marie did not look up and kept her face covered. Once or twice she seemed to shake her head sharply, as if saying no impatiently. Then she took a deep breath, lowered her hands and looked up at Greta. She was ashen except for two spots of red in her cheeks like rouge, though she wore none. Her eyelids drooped as if in deep fatigue. She opened her mouth to speak, there was a twitch to one side of her face, and she said softly, Beyeah.

Drink some water, Greta said. What's the matter?

Greta helped her with the water, some of which ran from one side of her mouth. Mrs Desir seemed able however to hold the glass firmly by herself. Greta then crouched by her side with an arm around her shoulders, trying to decide if Mrs Desir was unable or unwilling to say what had happened. Was she ill? Had she been harmed by someone? Greta positioned herself to look directly, clinically, into the woman's face, with the close scrutiny of a maid who has looked for trouble and dirt in every unknown corner.

Mrs Desir looked up. Now there were tears, tears it seemed of fright and pleading. Her hand clutched Greta's arm.

It's all right. Can you walk? I'll take you home.

By the time Greta had got her into bed, had drawn the curtains and lighted a fire in the hearth for visual comfort, Mrs Desir seemed herself again, though tired. Greta telephoned Mr Desir, who came immediately. When he entered the bedroom Marie sat up and turned with a false but effective brightness, as if to ask, Why have you come home? and even, Why ever am I in bed? She lay back against the pillows and looked at him.

What's this? John asked, and put his hand on her forehead.

It's nothing, she replied. I got a migraine at Hannigan's. She had a long history of migraines.

I was about to take one of those pills from Carson, she said. Immediately Greta went into the bathroom and reappeared with an open palm and a glass of water. Later, in the kitchen, Greta presented her version. She described the twitching, the inability to speak, how the water had dribbled from Marie's mouth.

And she cried, Greta said. She cried.

John had installed an elaborate intercom system in the house, and by pushing a button on the phone by her bed, Marie could listen to what was being said in the kitchen. Now she replaced the receiver carefully and gazed at the fire. She thought of her mother, who had been dead for many years. She thought she knew what had happened in the restaurant. But it was over now and it might never happen again.

But a few months later, while they were attending a boat-owners' convention in Miami, it all fell in on her. She awoke in the middle of the night seized by an unknown and horrible fear. She felt simultaneously a numbness here and a pain there, two feelings that seemed to exchange places. Getting out of bed, she fell noiselessly to the carpet, barely interrupting John's snoring. Her right leg was numb. She lay on the floor, unable to rise, unwilling to wake John, then pulled a blanket from the bed and covered herself. She lay there waiting for the light to come and for the numbness to go. At dawn she pulled herself into bed and fell deeply asleep. If anything it was John's cologne that woke her. He was dressed and on his way down to another meeting.

You have a luncheon with the women, don't you? he said, bending over her and stroking the side of her head the way he did sometimes.

She nodded, not wanting to chance a syllable, then closed her eyes sleepily. She awoke again a few hours later. The numbness was gone but her arm hurt, and when she spoke to her reflection in the mirror there was a lag between the forming of the words and the words—like an echo. The idea of missing the women's luncheon held for her the force of preemptive defeat, the loss of a battle barely drawn.

Except for one friend, she was seated at a circular table with nine strangers, the middle-aged wives of moderately successful men, all of whom owned either a sailboat or a powerboat. The theme of the convention was unrelievedly naval. The men wore uniforms and braided caps, were led by officers of the bridge. The woman Marie knew at the table wore a white middy blouse in a show of spirit. First the woman smiled across at her, then frowned at Marie's reaction—a lopsided smile that brought only half her face into play.

Holding Marie's own quizzical look with one of deep concern, the woman came around the table.

Marie, are you okay, dear?

Marie gave her the same smile, with her lips pressed together, and nodded, amid the din of four hundred ladies being seated. In these moments something in the left hemisphere of her brain was taking on charm, then form. Where it hadn't been it now was. The right side of her face twitched as cells winked out and went black. Her right eye blinked. The cords in her neck became taut. She looked down, away from her friend, a napkin raised to her lips.

Okay, Marie, it's all right honey, the woman said, and took Marie in her arms.

Some hours later his brother Jack telephoned him.

It's one of those calls, Max. It's Mom.

He flew to Miami that afternoon. When he came into the room she was sitting up, as if she were on a beach blanket instead of a hospital bed, with the same brightness, the same reassurance that this was not a catastrophe. She asked if he noticed a slight sag to one side of her mouth and he replied, yes, he could just make it out. He sat on the bed and held her hand. He looked around. Here was another hospital room. Outside the window, beyond the air conditioning and the wooden louvers, were the humidity, the palm trees, the flatness of Miami. Inside, all the orderlies were Cuban, all the patients elderly Jews. The lobby looked like a bank, everything was impeccable. The food in the cafeteria, he would discover, was delicious. No one can do this sort of thing like the Jews, his father said.

After a while the results of a cross-sectional scanner were brought in, which showed a lateral picture of Marie's brain, like a lemon slice, composed of the most total symmetry. Looking at it Max was unable to find anything out of place, any dot or dotlessness that did not have its counterpart. Then, when it was pointed out, he could see a short dark line of damage, like a scar or even a photographic fault. It indicated a small ruptured dam, with a flow of blood down a tiny valley, wiping out all inhabitants.

But virtually all of her speech returned by the third day. Possessed of a natural glibness, she seemed nearly as articulate as before. She told the story of waking in the middle of the night, the numbness, the luncheon, the seizure, her friend's reaction. The convention had ended the day after the incident and everyone had left. But at the Miami airport on their way home, suddenly the friend from the luncheon was there with her husband. The woman leaned over Marie's wheelchair, unable to hide her worry at how tired and drawn Marie looked. And for that moment, perhaps because she was startled, Marie was not able to speak very well. She stammered and the woman began to cry, then was embarrassed, murmured an excuse and rushed away, followed by her husband. Well, Marie said, looking up and widening her eyes.

An uneasy and artificial aura of the normal took hold. Everyone was aware of the illusion that nothing important had happened. In Max's mind, Dan's accident and coma, followed by his mother's stroke, was an indication of the beginning of a long progression, a spiral, a ripple effect. Each phase of the cycle led inexorably to the next.

One Easter, when they were children, his sister Robin was given a white duckling. For a few months they kept it indoors, in a carton littered with droppings and limp lettuce. When it was big enough they set it out on the river, like an ingenious toy that could float. It fitted immediately into a well-established flock of white ducks, former gifts, that lived on the river, and within a moment all of its graceless, carton-bound existence on land seemed obliterated. Afternoons, on his way home from school, Max would stop and try to pick out their duck from the others. To attract the flock one day he pulled bits of paper from his pocket, bits, he thought, of a candy wrapper. But as a few of the ducks and then the rest of the flock wafted over, he noticed the thrown bits were the wrong color; not brown but green. He was feeding money to the ducks. To retrieve the pieces, which anyway the ducks were rejecting with disdain, he took a rock from the water's edge and lobbed it into their midst. With a flurry of alarm they fled in a broken circle of escape, into the center of which, like an overplayed force of destruction, the rock fell. The ducks slid away, certain of them turning to look at him closely, as if to memorize the face and form of such treachery. But the bits of money were gone, and Max, filled with remorse, stood on the grassy bank watching the ripples widen. Five or six concentric circles were followed by smaller ones in a diminishing series, which slid smoothly across the water and disappeared.

Three weeks after returning from Miami, Marie had another seizure. She was taken to the hospital in Manhattan, one floor up from Dan's old floor and identical to it. Her symptoms this time were more pronounced—a limp and numbness on the right side, serious aphasia and forgetfulness, and a feeling of complete fatigue.

The doctor called them all together. He said he was sorry. It was not a stroke but a tumor, located in the center of Marie's brain and therefore inoperable. She might live another six months, perhaps longer. The name was glioblastoma; he expected it would grow quickly. He said that radiation therapy would have some effect, would extend her life for a time, six months, perhaps a year; although with side effects. She will lose her hair, he said. I suggest you make arrangements to get a wig.

Max went home. He did not cry until he filled the bathtub and got into it. It was an amniotic bath. If somehow he could have filled the room itself with water, with rain, with billowing steam, he would have. When the tears burned his eyes he slid beneath the surface. He was calmed, as if he had drowned, except that the water flowed out, not in, a drowning in reverse. When he stood up and saw his reflection in the mirror, he realized the danger he was in. Everyone was sick and dying: his mother, his uncle Dan, perhaps himself and anyone else who came too close. It was a force that drew him in, or on its own drew near. In her present state of sedation his mother seemed suddenly to have caught up with Dan. She might not outlive him.

John told Marie what Dr Feeney had said. The word tumor was avoided. It was something in her head; although some weeks later she herself said the word to Max. Nor did John tell her about the prognosis of six months, mainly, Max thought, because John could not make himself believe it. Nor did he say, You are dying. Several times during those days, however, she forced out the words herself—I want to die, I want to die. She said it when she cried, as a kind of keening that made Max think of all the generations of women who had taught her these reactions.

He called about the wig and made an appointment. She went in a wheelchair, wearing a wide-brimmed straw hat and dark glasses—the radiation caused an extreme sensitivity to the sun—a costume that made her seem romantic and powerful. Mutely she commanded cars, arrangements, appointments, deference, respect. The proprietor, whose name was Romeo, led them into a mirrored cubicle. Here there were six or seven Maxes, Maries, Johns and Romeos; although Marie, whose chair was aimed at the big mirror in front of her, hardly took her eyes from her principal reflection, as if this sight, at such a close, well-lighted range, came as a sudden surprise, causing disbelief or a startling new fear that soon she would be unrecognizable even to herself. After some discussion Romeo produced a gray wig with a single-length, spiky, lifeless look. He placed it on a wooden stock and within a few minutes had given it the general configurations of Marie's hair, minus the curl and a certain lightness of color, a silvery gray she'd been cultivating for years. Then he combed her own hair back and placed the wig on her head.

Max saw the color rise in her cheeks. The wig sat too low on her forehead, and stood out in a single unconvincing fingerwave at the nape of her neck. Suddenly she was a very old woman. Her eyes went to Max in a precise ricochet off the mirror. Romeo stepped out of the cubicle to choose another pair of scissors, and John, who had been standing in the doorway of the tiny room, stepped back to let him pass. Marie's eyes seemed to plead with Max to be her witness, to remember that while she was one thing now, with her drooping mouth and lined skin reflected around her in fifty ways, the fake hair like a comical hat on her head, that she once had been so much another: lovely, vivacious and young, and perfectly at home in a room of mirrors.

He took her hand. There was nothing to say, no gallantries, no lies, no explanations of how this could have happened; no excuses, no compensations. It became simply a question of whether she was going to cry in front of a stranger. She drew in a sharp breath and blinked. Romeo returned. He promised that when it was finished, the wig would suit her. When he offered his hand as they were leaving, she pressed it to her cheek.

Later, Max accompanied her to the radiotherapy lab in a slab-walled, subbasement of the hospital. She lay on a table with wheels, her head taped in place, a black dot marked in ink on her temple. He was disappointed to learn that the huge machine was twelve years old, although still considered effective. The nurses retreated behind a lead door as if into a bunker at the height of an air raid. He regarded his mother on the television monitor. She held herself absolutely still. He had an elaborate fantasy—of her health returning, of a trip to Mexico for radical cosmetic surgery. Miraculously she would be restored to herself, to that woman from the past who, one summer day, driving home, had looked over and said, Let's stop at the farm and get some peaches. I'll bet they're sweet as sugar.

It was June. They brought her home from the hospital. She lay wrapped in a blanket on a chaise in the garden. She drowsed, listening to the birds. The big house, white and luminous in the spring air, gave off sounds—a whisper from the sliding door as they checked on her, voices within, doors, bells. The house and its trees loomed up around her, over a ledge of terrace and flowers. The fresh, leafy air had a percussive silence, a quality of distant padded sound that wafted across the parklike yards of neighboring lives.

She fell brink to brink down a well of sleep. Her uncle Leo, with tight red hair and rolled sleeves, confronted her at the top of the stairs. She was sixteen. Where have you been? he said. She stopped two steps below him. At the pictures with my friends. Mama knew.

Don't lie! he shouted. It's already dark. You've been with a boy! He raised his hand to strike her and she fell backward down the narrow flight of stairs. She lay at the bottom listening to two things—her uncle's howls of anguish, and something else, something smaller: a buzz like an insect in her ear. Was that the first time she heard it? Her uncle Leo again appeared before her, this time with white boxes of sweets from the bakery. She cried out and swatted him away. In a moment Robin was saying, Mom, wake up, Mom. And Marie looked up into her daughter's eyes and thought to say, Do you remember, Robin, when I asked you to hold your head next to mine and listen closely? Do you remember that buzzing you heard? But this question came out only in her eyes, so that Robin said, What is it, Mom? Can I get you something?

Chocolates, Marie thought, and said aloud, Chaucer. Robin took her hand and said she didn't understand. Marie closed her eyes again. She sat at a little table in a large, high-ceilinged shop, amid forty such tables, at each of which sat a woman or young girl like herself, her hair in a net, wearing a white apron, one hand resting in her lap. With the other hand Marie took a little ball of mocha candy and rolled it in a tray of melted chocolate in front of her. She could fashion fifteen a minute; a delicate crossover loop at each tip, the thick smell of sugar in the air, one of the women a few tables over saying, Dammit, it's hot, my loops are melting.

❦ ────────────────────────────────────

Marie threw off the blanket and turned her face to cooler air. Robin said, You're warm. Would you like some juice? Marie reached up and touched her daughter's face.

It seemed they were going on ahead without her. Wasn't that it? They were leaving her behind. They were all so far off from her now that she saw them only when they presented themselves, when they came right up and put their faces a few inches from her eyes.

Mama? It was Max. I'm going now, he said. I'll be back to see you tomorrow. She nodded her head and he kissed her. She looked behind him and saw other faces. A row of people sat there in a semicircle. Well! she said. What *is* this?

What is what? Max said.

Them! she thought, but she said, vehemently, I! She had meant also to point behind him for emphasis, but her right arm only jerked up weakly in a spasm, like a dreaming animal.

She sighed deeply. Penny and her little girl came up beside Max and leaned over her. Marie could see that Penny's smile was the rueful kind. The little girl was awed.

Penny said, Give Nanny a kiss. A delicate, blond cheek hovered without touching hers, then withdrew. Marie rifled through her mind as through a bin of old clothes. Amanda. The child's name was Amanda.

Mandy, she said clearly, and held out her left hand. Mandy returned and this time firmly planted a kiss on her grandmother's cheek. Was that right? Marie thought, and raised her eyebrows inquisitively at Max.

She dreamed often of Dan. They said hello to each other at the beginning of each dream. Or they called to each other until they met in the context of the dream—in a field, on a beach, or in a room they had played in as children. In the dreams Dan had lost something, a penknife with an ivory handle. She helped him look for it, in the field, on the beach, under the snow. They never found it. She saw him down on the ground, a young boy now, searching in the grass.

That knife is lost, she said. Why don't you give up?

Dan didn't answer. He never answered.

II

MARIE TOLD MAX THIS STORY:

In 1907 young Danilo Defilippo, Marie's father, was walking through a sewing factory owned by his family in Messina when he noticed a beautiful girl working at one of the tables. In those days in Sicily, and given the difference in their lives, the only next step in his interest in her was a proposal of marriage. He was, however, already engaged to a young woman of means from Calabria, directly across the Straits of Messina. Danilo didn't love this woman but had been prepared to marry her because she was pleasant, agreeable and rich. Her family and his had formed a marriage pool for several generations, and in a complicated way they were cousins. Her dowry would include three hundred acres of forest in Calabria. For years artisans there had painted wood to look like marble. Now trees were scarce and they painted marble to look like wood. Danilo and this Calabrian would already have been married if the forest in question had not recently caught fire and burned, necessitating a postponement of the marriage and further talks between the families.

The beautiful girl in the factory was named Angela Leone. She was tall and fair with green eyes, and her people had been fishermen. Her parents were dead but her brother Leo eagerly agreed to the match and gave her away.

Danilo and Angela were married in 1908 amid a flap of intricate ritual accompanied by family disappointment amounting to indignation. Angela of course brought no dowry. Even the clothes on her back were unsuitable. To Danilo's three sisters in particular this marriage to a poor peasant was catastrophic. They cursed the fact that their Calabrian cousin's forest had burned and even pictured Angela racing wild-eyed through the flaming trees with a torch.

Max was curious about the idea that Angela would stop the marriage by burning her rival's forest. What did that mean? Could she ever have been thought capable of such a thing? Her saints did it for her, Marie said. Angela's saints fought the Calabrian girl's saints and won.

But there was nothing romantic or ethereal about the new bride. To the genteel Defilippo sisters Angela was exuberant and coarse. They misunderstood her as if she were foreign; they were ungenerous and at times plainly rude. Angela did her best to appease them, but a streak of obstinance sometimes caused her to flaunt the traits they despised.

For the honeymoon Danilo took her to Florence and Rome, her first trip anywhere. With him Angela was quiet and even graceful. The sisters had seen to it that she was beautifully dressed. Now she realized that demureness in a first-class train or hotel passed for breeding. She could be demure, although she was taller than her husband and felt dishonest at it. The honeymoon was a trip to another world, another life; of afternoons of love in hotels, of parks and bell towers, long carriage rides and antiquities, a softer sunshine. They returned to Messina just two weeks before the great earthquake of 1908, a catastrophe that reduced the city to rubble, flattening it as if with bombs. Seventy-five thousand people died; and among the Defilippos two of Danilo's brothers, many in-laws, cousins, countless friends. Every family had its stories of disaster. Destroyed in the quake were the large Defilippo house in the city, several businesses connected with the family, the sewing factories and warehouses, odd pieces of real estate, and a white stone villa, called *Contemplazione*, which overlooked the straits from a promontory outside the city.

Angela sat on the terrace with most of the family for an outdoor lunch, dreamily describing to a young cousin a night at the Rome Opera. Then someone said, Oh Dio, what's that! and every head went up. Suddenly a gigantic cracking sound split the air, like hundreds of lightning bolts hitting trees. The terrace and the ground beneath it began to shake. Plates and glasses fell and broke on the stone. A deep, terrifying rumble rolled along under everything. Out in front of the villa, halfway across the straits, the sea floor split, and water from both sides rushed into the fissure. They saw a boat go into the rising steam as if over a waterfall. The water was swirling and black, the steam rose up, and high on the terrace their faces were drenched with a hot mist. Now the split appeared on the beach, like an animal coming out of the water; it began to move up the hill toward the villa. The women screamed. They picked up the children and ran. The whole family ran. The fissure moved up the hill and under the house, which fell open like a cantaloupe.

In the city everything that could fall, fell. There followed days and weeks of fires, disease, of digging out the traumatized survivors, the mutilated dead. On the third day, one of the three Defilippo sisters was found in the rubble of her house, her two babies in her arms, one of them dead; and her husband, also dead, nearby. Concetta, whose arm and leg were broken, had fed her child on the scattered remains of another grossly interrupted lunch.

Marie was born a year later; a second girl named Victoria died in infancy. Marie's earliest memories were of visits to this child's crypt in the Defilippo mausoleum, a horror of nineteenth-century Sicilian gloom, tastelessly spared by the earthquake. Its centerpiece was a glass coffin containing the preserved remains of her grandmother, Danilo's mother, then in her twentieth year of eternity. Every fifth anniversary of her death, her breakaway gown was changed and her hair carefully dusted. Then the glass case was resealed and a deafening compressor sucked out the useless air.

In the spring of 1913, when Marie was four, Danilo was forced by the threat of a second conscription into the Italian Army to flee the country. After Unification, the government had made a late and disorganized effort to colonize. Everywhere small wars, which were not strictly legal, were being fought with mercenaries and what remnants of the Army could be spared: in North Africa, the Aegean, in Turkey where the Ottoman Empire was coming apart like the hassock with which henceforth it would always be associated. An uncle who was a general advised Danilo to flee rather than certainly and foolishly risk his life a second time. To be sent to any of the fronts meant death. He left one night by boat for Genoa, from there sailing on the White Star Line to New York. He planned a stay of six months, or until his uncle and other friends could rearrange affairs to permit his return.

❧ ———————————————————————

Max wondered also about this part of the story. Why was it necessary for his grandfather to go all the way to America? Why not have gone to London, or over the Alps to Switzerland? People came to America to stay, not to visit. Perhaps he had chosen New York as an adventure, to cover the anguish of leaving Angela and Marie behind.

With their brother gone the Defilippo sisters closed in on Angela like cats. This was their chance and they knew it. Until then they had brought a certain restraint to their criticism, Angela being after all the future *capo*'s wife, peasant or not. But now they complained about everything, her habits, her manners, the way she talked. She had one idiosyncrasy, a hobby she refused to give up, which infuriated the sisters and sent them rushing in a rage from window to window of the villa, which like everything else had been rebuilt after the earthquake. Angela liked to fish. Her father and grandfather had been fishermen. Both had drowned. She fished and thought of them.

Occasionally, in fine weather, she would dress as she had before her marriage, and with tackle from a boathouse under the terrace, would fish incognita from some rocks nearby. She knew this was wrong, that sometimes the three sisters wept with indignation and shame and broke things. But she didn't fish often, and always went out early, just after dawn. She stood barefoot on the rocks, holding the rod like a parade flag, her skirts hitched up to her knees, as the sun rose, a deep vermilion ball over Calabria. Afterward, for the sisters, came the worst part. Angela would scale and clean the fish herself, and cook it in a kitchen full of servants who thought her crazy. Behind her back she was called *La Pescatora*, the fishwife. If somehow the sisters could have arranged, through some magnificent bargain, to have her struck by lightning while she fished from the rocks, they'd have done so.

One morning when Danilo had been gone several months, Angela entered the kitchen with her catch and found the three sisters waiting. This time it was they who carried on like fishwives, while the servants stood about fascinated. Concetta, who had been crippled in the earthquake, so that each year she seemed to grow smaller and more gnarled, was the most vicious.

You bring us nothing but shame and smelly fish, she cried in a small, high, monkey voice. The other two joined in. You smell of fish. You reek. Who knows what you do in the boathouse . . .

Angela stood in the doorway holding an eel and three sea bass tied together at the gills. Four-year-old Marie, who had gone out with her mother, stood at her side.

Do you think it's right for the little girl to watch her mother play on the rocks? Concetta screeched. She will grow up to be trash like you.

The raised voices, the hate in the room, caused the child to cry and Angela, who had said nothing, patted her on the head. Then, taking the cluster of fish in both hands, she rushed at the sisters with a cry, swatting at them wildly as they screamed and ran about the kitchen. She chased them and hit at them until the fish came apart and the sisters were battered to the floor.

That afternoon she piled all her opulent wedding gifts into a cart, which she dragged to town and sold for passage money to New York, one way, for herself and Marie. They were gone within hours, and Angela never in her life saw any of the Defilippos again. She arrived with Marie on Ellis Island, Danilo's name and address pinned to their lapels. He came to claim them, stunned, exhilarated by the madness, the irretrievability of the act. Angela said she would never go back. They would stay forever in New York, become Americans.

On the advice of earlier arrivals, Danilo had rented two rooms in the Italian section on the Lower East Side of Manhattan. He had suffered a torment of homesickness that was not completely alleviated by Angela's arrival with Marie. What of the others and his connection and responsibility to them? Nor did he like New York, with its noise, crowds and expense. Half of the money he had brought with him was gone. He felt he had been trapped. He, who at home would have directed two factories of garment workers, now became a local tailor, one of hundreds. Instead of the comfortable life they might have led in Messina, surrounded by a substantial family—the life he had offered Angela—they lived now at her station, as immigrants, working hard and keeping to themselves. After a time he stopped asking her to go back. And then she was pregnant again and all thoughts of returning to Messina were dropped. After Danilo, Jr, came a third and last child, Franco—Dan and Frank as Marie called them. She was twelve when they moved to Brooklyn, to Avenue U, a comfortable Italian neighborhood where customs were similar to what they'd have been in Messina, if in an American mode. They shopped from the same horse-drawn carts, the same *pasticcerias*. Everyone spoke Italian, in various dialects; only the children learned English, or had contact with people who were different.

From the beginning letters came from Messina, begging Danilo to return, to enjoy what was his. But Angela said she would die first. In Messina she was nothing. Here everyone was nothing, which was at least something. The letters brought news, gossip and occasionally a photograph, an elaborate production, like a picture still from an opera or the beginning of a painting with props, and a gaze held so long as to have taken on alarming individuality and presence. Danilo sent back pictures of his own. One showed Marie, Angela and him sitting in a little, thin-masted skiff, before a painted backdrop of an Italian lake. On the back of the photograph, which later Marie had enlarged, she wrote: Summer 1913, Marie four years old, Mom twenty-three, Dad twenty-eight. It was the first picture Danilo sent to Messina. Perhaps the three of them in the little boat was meant to show that they had all made it safely to the other side.

He sent other pictures that later Max saw in Messina, of Marie in school—Clara Bow had infected them all with perfect mouths—of Dan and Frank, first in their playsuits and later in the uniform of the American Army; of John and Marie in their engagement and wedding pictures, in which Marie is turned to look over her train as if over a savanna of white satin. After the war started the letters from Italy changed. An evolving smugness was replaced by uncertainty, then anxiety, then fear and need. Could Danilo send food and medicine? Throughout the neighborhood in Brooklyn people were receiving similar requests. Please send penicillin. Send food. Italy was sick and starving.

The post office prescribed measurements for the packages and Danilo made them of heavy cloth to save weight. Rather than use twine he masterfully sewed them shut. More of the family wrote to ask for help—in-laws, cousins. Packages went out every week. He sent everything he could. After a time the requests were for different things, less of necessity than of opportunity; not just food but particular foods; not just clothes but a red dress, a blue scarf. Angela wanted to know why she and her children were sacrificing to buy material for red dresses and blue scarves. Danilo said he would stop sending the packages when they began asking for wristwatches. Which they did, and he did.

In 1948, after the war, thirty-five years after leaving it, Danilo returned to Messina for a stay of three months. He was sixty-three. He asked Angela to accompany him this last time but she refused. In the three decades of letters from Sicily they had never mentioned her by name. Dan, Frank and Marie were all married and could not go, nor would they have wanted to; and so Danilo went alone.

He had not quite understood the necessity or effect of the packages of food and medicine. For long periods of the war twenty or thirty of the family had lived on nothing else. Specifically, the penicillin had saved the lives of three of them. When he stepped off the boat train in Messina everyone was there, forming a crowd which at first he took to be travelers going to the mainland. They saw him and called his name. Then he recognized certain faces, older and changed, like music played slower. He saw their tears, their outstretched arms, and nearly swooned in the overwhelming embrace of family.

He stayed the summer, living at once an exaggerated and abbreviated version of the life he had missed. He sat on the terrace of *Contemplazione* looking out over the balustrade at the sea, at the long low rise of Calabria, where the forests had burned. He had come back because his life was nearly over. He wanted to see how it had happened that he, out of all of them, had become separated from the others. Why had he not hid elsewhere, or somehow convinced Angela to return, or simply gone off and fought in Turkey? Would he so easily have been killed? Why had his whole life kept him from where he belonged?

He wondered what he had missed. What point had

tnere been to it other than the vague supposition that flight had saved his life and was therefore the essential fact of his existence? To have survived elsewhere was better than dying here, he supposed, but at the price of exile. He realized that for the past thirty-five years he had been someone and something other than that which at this moment he had again become. Sitting on the terrace of *Contemplazione*, he felt at last transported into the center of the endless daydream that had filled all his hours and years of sewing. *What were they like? What were they doing? Did they think of him?*

He visited the mausoleum to see the crypts of his mother and the daughter who had died in infancy. He could not remember his mother in life. Her corpse had eclipsed whatever existence she had led, both in memory and in actual years; she was now much older in death than she had been in life, and was remembered only for her conspicuousness—a grotesque waxen doll to replace the sweet, vague softness of recollection. The glass coffin was intact although they no longer changed her gown or replenished the vacuum, and the rictus of a kind of imminent scream—like a sneer—seemed to have claimed the lips. But the flesh was uncorrupted, the hair was dark and seemed firmly attached to the scalp; and altogether, as an artifact, the mummy provided Danilo with what he most needed—a reminder of the fact, or of the illusion, that this object had once been his mother, but was no more.

This was the story Marie told Max.

Marie Defilippo met John Desiderio at the engagement party of a mutual friend. John's sister Clara had been a classmate of hers and Marie knew about the Desiderios, a large poor family of five sons and two daughters who lived a few blocks away on Avenue J.

❦ ───────────────────────────

John was black-haired and blue-eyed, thanks to the Norman conquest of Caltanissetta one sunny afternoon and the rape of all its women; he was tall, handsome, ambitious and given to a certain flashiness of style. Marie caught his eye at once. She wore a peach satin dinner gown with a low back that her father had made for her, as he made all her clothes. She had always been dressed like a princess. At fourteen she had had a coat trimmed with ermine tails. Her dark hair was piled on her head. The other girls beside her were naturally pretty in some cases, plain or unappealing in others, but with none of Marie's fineness. John saw immediately she was the kind of woman who could help him better himself.

He took her to a fine restaurant in Manhattan, having hired a car for the occasion. Until then it had been a question of his choosing. Anyone who knew him could see all he had to do was choose; no girl would ever fail to say yes. But then he removed her wrap and saw the way she sat, the way the waiter thought she was rich and showed it. He realized he might not be able to do without her. She was what he needed, it seemed, more than she needed him.

Three separate things might have kept her from accepting him: he was a year younger than she, he was an amateur boxer, and she was nearly engaged to another man. Later, when she told these things to Max, she was quite proud of the fact that this other man had also made something of himself and become rich. At eighteen, John had begun a boxing career with a middleweight Golden Gloves championship and a manager who had him file his teeth—dull or sharp, Max never knew. He lied to Marie about his age, quit boxing, and kept company with her for a year, paying the kind of devotional and polite court that

Danilo Defilippo insisted upon for his daughter the *principessa mancata*.

In 1934, John paid seven hundred and fifty dollars for a honeymoon trip on the *Rotterdam* to Bermuda—this at the height of the Depression. To the neighbors in Brooklyn, it was as if they had gone to the moon. The trip was one of a series of grand, impulsive moves, of a generous, confident and unprotected nature, and part of an overall attitude of promise and ambition by which John had convinced her of his seriousness and won her. In a sequence of snapshots from the honeymoon, Marie is poised on a rock in the surf, carrying on like Rita Hayworth; then by the ship's rail, dressed for the afternoon in a cloche hat; dapper John in gray by the same rail, before a bleached-out sea. They returned home and moved out of Brooklyn, tracing their parents' steps back to Manhattan. This it seemed was the way out of the maze. Then across the river to New Jersey, the Hudson River having seemed nearly as wide as the Atlantic, and as difficult to cross.

They lived in an apartment at the top of an old house in Englewood, on a quiet, tree-lined street, the first of three suburban arrangements they would have together over the next forty years, this one the simplest, with dimity curtains and painted chairs in the kitchen, a white chenille spread on the bed. Marie was soon pregnant with John, Jr. She walked to town for exercise until the seventh, nearly the eighth month. Many women seemed to be pregnant and out walking. John found work as the underforeman of a local distillery. He invited the foreman home to dinner, to meet Marie. She did not understand he was a foreman and thought him very young to be so influential. She asked him why he hadn't brought his young lady and he replied that he had not been as lucky in life as John; he had no young lady.

Subsequently, the foreman invited John for a drink after work. They discussed their ambitions; the foreman gave John advice. John suggested a new system of inventory, a new arrangement of certain of the bottling machines. They had a few drinks although John disliked liquor and was impervious to its effects. The foreman, however, quickly got drunk. Hanging on John's neck he said what a helluva guy he was, an Italian stud. John pushed him away and left. Sometime later John went to the distillery after hours to retrieve something and heard voices in the changing room. He discovered the foreman and the night watchman having sex. The foreman had his pants down around his ankles and was leaning over the sink. John had been unaware of this biological possibility between men and was nauseated by the discovery.

The watchman was dismissed, the foreman resigned and John was promoted. He worked there for five more years; then in 1939 took a much better job as plant manager of a company that made a mild tonic for the liver with a national reputation based on discreet advertising and a certain unproved placebo effect. It was the president of the tonic company who suggested that John shorten his name from Desiderio to Desir. Marie thought the idea shameful but yielded to the force of the argument—Italians were greaseballs then—and the beauty of the new name. She enjoyed the sound of Marie Desir. It had bothered her to have to spell out Desiderio all the time. The name was legally changed, for themselves and for Jack, and Robin—Roberta—who had just been born. When the next child came Marie was determined to compensate for the loss of three vowels with an Italian first name. Massimo Desir was born in 1941. John, however, neatly outmaneuvered Marie by calling the baby Max, a name she disliked because it sounded German. You can't win, she said.

By the time their last child—named Angela but called Penny—was born in 1943, they had moved from Englewood and settled comfortably into their penultimate house, in their penultimate town in New Jersey— Indian River. They all lived there for the next twenty-five years.

III

THE HOUSE IN INDIAN RIVER HAD A TALL GABLE IN FRONT, two balconies, and a large chimney that rose up its back like a spine. It had been built in 1936, was made of brick, and was surrounded by enormous old trees. The street on which it was a corner house, was paved with white concrete squares edged with tar, like a Mondrian, and was covered over with a canopy of linden branches. Many of these trees were eventually lost but Max could remember when they lined both sides of the street with a grand, antebellum regularity.

Marie and John had chosen the town carefully. Indian River had pre-Revolutionary touches. General Washington had come through from Valley Forge on his way to fight the Battle of New York, and had forded the river at a point now given over to canoeing in summer and skating in winter. The river meandered through town with an exaggerated indolence, making seven major turns back on itself. When you went to town or came home from school you crossed the river two or three times. In the nineteenth century this meandering had inspired the mayor and aldermen to sponsor an annual water festival, with extravagant floats and fireworks on the river, with competitions, games, bake-offs and concerts on the banks. Sousa came. When Max was fifteen the festival was revived for one year. It was held in Indian Park on and around the lake, where the river either started out or ended up, depending on your view; with extravagant floats, fireworks, competitions, games, bake-offs, concerts. A large rocket misfired and fell into the crowd, badly burning several people and putting out the eye of a child. The river was just as it had been, while everything else had changed.

Indian River was on a planet different from the one that had produced the Lower East Side. When John's family came to visit they were stiff, though momentarily jocular in front of a camera, and dressed either too warmly or too well. They brought white boxes of sweet cookies and cannoli. In their minds this was the country, ineffably American. They were back in the city by dark.

Besides the park and the winding river, the end of town where Max lived was bordered by farmland—expanses of fields and meadows, of blank spaces from another era, where the tops of hills and trees met the sky and the air smelled of grass and turned earth. He and the dog played in the woods, the same as if he had been born a thousand miles to the west and fifty years earlier; except that as they grew the town grew. By the end of his childhood the farmland was gone. He and his friends found a dead cat one afternoon, and after dragging it in a wagon from house to house to find its owner, stuffed it between the walls of a house under construction, on the site of a tree fort they had taken great care to build. Subsequently a man and his wife moved in and made their local reputation on the strength of a new device that opened their garage door automatically.

John and Marie's bedroom had a fireplace and two closets, one in each corner of the same wall, his father's on the left and his mother's on the right. They were apparently equal, and each occupied the isosceles space created by the dormer roof. But to Max, perhaps because of the difference in clothes—the colorful, silky, voluminous folds of dresses compared to the prosaic hangings, hats, ties and shoes neatly arranged—it seemed that his father's side contained less space; as if, he concluded one day, a part of it had been set aside for something secret, a space perhaps, or a tiny hidden room. It was as if Max were trying to enhance the house, by giving it something he thought the pink mansion at the end of the street must have. And later, in discovering that an ornate brass andiron in the fireplace had a loose piece to it that swiveled, he imagined this was the switch that opened the secret place in his father's closet. In his mind he saw a little panel snap open, to reveal a small dark interior space just behind the suits and hats. In it would be the implements of another life, in another world.

He and the dog were nearly the same age. When he was sixteen Max was told to have him put to sleep. He considered the suggestion for three days. Everything had slowed down between them but they were brothers. Somehow it was a test. John and Marie wanted to involve him directly so that afterward there would be no recriminations.

Max took him. The dog sat trembling on the seat of the car. It was over in a few minutes. The dog went to sleep and was gone. As he was driving away Max looked over his shoulder and saw the veterinarian's assistant put something the right color into a smoking incinerator. It was five o'clock in the afternoon. He drove home and

went up to the attic, where lately he'd been experiment-
ing with oil paints. He pulled the room apart, slashed the
canvases, squirted oil paints on the wall, wept. Down in
the kitchen Marie and John—who had just come home
from work and wanted to know what was going on—
wondered if they had done the right thing.

Summers they rented a succession of cottages in a succession of resorts on the New Jersey shore. This they had
done since Max and Penny were born, before the resorts
were completely established, when all the men were away
and blackout curtains covered the windows under bright
starry nights. Home movies in fact showed a time of stark
simplicity, with two or three striped umbrellas in acres of
white empty beach; of women alone with their children,
squinting into the sun without dark glasses. Max holds
Penny's hand at the water's edge. They are four and
three. The shot is not staged; in another that is, Marie
twirls in front of the camera in a new bathing suit with a
short skirt. She looks in turn over each of her raised
shoulders and extends her arms down and back, in a pose
she had lately seen a model strike in the Pathé News. Her
hair is long and sepia-colored. She is thirty-six, one year
younger than Max is now.
    Winters, at Christmas, all of Marie's family and
some of John's came to stay overnight. Uncle Frank did
magic tricks and carried on. After midnight Mass they
had potatoes and eggs and the adults stayed up the rest of
the night playing pinochle, not only because they enjoyed
cards but because there weren't enough beds for everyone to sleep in at once. A diagram was posted on the refrigerator. Max slept in the attic, part of which had been
made into an irregular room covered with the kind of
paper used to line Victorian toy boxes. A space heater,
with crisscrossing V's of red coils, sent out a thin metallic

hum. The sheets were ice. A red glow filled the peaked space. Max and two or three cousins, at the top of the house like the detail at the top of a painting, warmed the beds for their uncles, who would pass them on the stairs in the early morning, stubble on their chins, their eyes shot with fatigue. Each year, as John progressed, the array of gifts was more dazzling. At thirteen, Max was given a Schwinn bicycle that was extremely beautiful although it had fat tires and took great strength to pedal. He'd been dreaming recurrently of a white horse for three or four years. It had got to and beyond the point of medical, if not outright psychological consultation. When John and Marie went out for the evening or away on a trip, they would return with a small equine statuette. Max had upward of twenty of them. The year of the Schwinn was the year he most completely expected the unreasonable gift of a live horse. He had thought it through. Half of the large detached garage would make a stall. The farm and fields lay just up the road.

The horse that came to collect him at night on the ledge outside his window was white. Max and his brother Jack shared a bedroom; on half the nights Jack had to tell him to get back in bed. The horse was a presence, benign and strong. Max stepped from the ledge onto his back and they flew off. They traveled together, nothing could be simpler. In the mornings, at a doctor's urging, Marie inquired into the latest excursion as if Max had just come in from the airport. And he would reply, An island to the south, the local hills, a place where there was snow on the ground. He thought he saw through the inquiries but liked sharing the experiences. Meanwhile his collection of horse statuettes grew. Some were of porcelain, some of bronze, a few of wood. He kept them on a shelf by his bed. The psychiatrist, interchangeable in John's and Marie's opinion with, in this case, a quack hypnotist—

who in the end only made Max's eyes water—had suggested a process of transference as a way out of the dilemma. But the dreams went on, the travels continued; the relationship with the white horse, rather than becoming externalized into any or all of the statuettes, existed independently of them. The horse was his, a benevolent creature that came from a place inaccessible to everyone else—his own dreams. He knew he imagined the horse; it was the imagining that made it real.

Once he took one of the statuettes outdoors, a substantial mistake. It was not the having of the statuettes that activated the transference but the use to which they were put. It was not possible to control the image of the horse when imposed on the gorgeous and banal reality of the morning, amid a number of rocks and a tree stump in the back yard that approximated Monument Valley. Being called upon to move from one place to another, the horse could not bend its legs or move its head. Max turned it over in his hand and looked at it closely. This was a bronze statuette and not a very good one; he had won it himself in the amusement park at the beach. He stood up and hurled it deep into the woods across the street where eventually the Costas built their house. He retrieved the statuette, but never played with any of them again. This particular bronze is the last one still in his possession, only because it was subsequently separated from the herd.

It was the Schwinn finally that banished the dream horse, which perhaps had only meant freedom and mobility. Riding the bike provided many of the same sensations as the dream. It seemed at the time that his disappointment and embarrassment at finding the Schwinn beside the tree—the gleaming approximation of his dream instead of its prancing embodiment—was a failure that caused the horse to flee, for after that Christmas it never appeared to him again.

He did, also, about this time, take up with live horses. He and his friend Scott, similarly passionate about similar things, rode up to a range of foothills within cycling distance, to a livery stable with energetic horses and endless trails. It was not the same as in his dreams. The horses were not interested in taking him places, or in being cloudlike and mysterious. He fell off, and once was nearly crushed when a huge bay went down on its knees, put its head back and began to roll over, Max, saddle and all. He stepped off, waited for the horse to right itself, then got back on—a parenthetical lapse, over in a moment; to the horse, this time, Max was the bewildering illusion.

🌳

Beneath one of the outdoor balconies was a flagstone terrace and cutting garden in which Marie had planted pansies, asters, zinnias, dahlias. This was overhung with the lacy leaves of two large white birches and an immense oak that later was blown down in a storm. His older sister Robin is sitting on a wooden bench, dressed in white as a young angel of the church. It is the day of her confirmation and of Max's first holy communion. Marie stands behind Robin brushing her long chestnut hair. The sun strikes the nimbus of white through the leaves. The dog is barking up at Max on the balcony. Marie looks up, the brush in her hand, and smiles. In her smile, he thinks, is the awareness of one of the pure, perfect moments of her life.

In a home movie of that day's dual ceremonies, the

white line snakes up the steps of the church, segments of little boys interlaced with segments of little girls, hands clasped around white prayerbooks and nosegays of tiny flowers. The wind lifts the girl's veils here and there in sudden soundless diaphanous explosions. Max appears. He looks into his father's camera. His face is blanched by the enormity of the occasion. He does not think he is ready to receive the Host. The large limestone church is new, its construction due largely to John Desir's inspired fund-raising. This double ceremony has been delayed for its completion. The vestibule smells of fresh cement, dank stone, lilies. It has nauseated Max. The moisture from his hands has loosened the cover of his prayerbook. Unlike the other boys he is wearing long pants, to cover the bandages on his legs. He remembers the stiff-legged constriction of climbing the steps outside the church, but the camera does not pick that up.

Marie bandaged him every night for long periods during the winter, using soft old sheets rolled into strips and stored neatly in the drawer of his night table, in rows, like little mounds of baker's dough. If he wasn't bandaged at night he scratched his arms and legs; in the morning they would be bleeding and raw. At St John's in the winter season, he wore white gloves. Sometimes Marie put long black socks up over his arms at night, turning them back into feet. In the mornings he wished for a slide that could take him down the stairs without having to bend his knees. Entering the kitchen he wondered that no one else must face this sort of thing. Apart from the hypnotist—a last resort—he was taken each year to a different doctor. No one could say why he had the affliction, which had appeared when he was a few weeks old, an eczema that covered his body up to the neck. Because of the bandages he didn't walk until he was nearly four. In the summer at the beach it left him, and came back in the fall. After his twelfth or thirteenth year less reappeared each time.

The white gloves occasioned rude remarks at school. They were of thin cotton, to be used once and thrown away, the left identical to the right and worn upside down. During this period all four children were sent down the street to the pink mansion for piano lessons. Mrs Watson suggested Max's lessons be discontinued, complaining of blood on her piano keys, an image she herself knew to be Romantic, but which might not be right for the child.

But by the time he was six they noticed he tapped his feet to the music, the bandages notwithstanding. Friday evenings before the era of television, John gave them lessons in ballroom dancing. Everyone of the older generation could dance—intricate, sophisticated maneuvers; the Peabody, the Montmartre (pronounced Mo-Mart), the Lindy, the Black Bottom. Max learned the steps easily, but it was the syncopation of tap he liked. Marie thought he needed something of his own. In the fourth grade he began private lessons at the Phyllis Weeks School of the Dance, downtown near the railway trestle, across from Calloway's Drugstore.

His first performance, of a routine he had just been taught, was for his own fourth-grade classmates at St John's on St Valentine's Day. After lunch the desks were arranged in a large circle. A record and phonograph in the coatroom sounded quite actual, like a real piano in the next room. The children, untouched by TV, were naïvely appreciative. When he finished, Sister Margaret noticed that one of his leg bandages had come unraveled; the end of it snaked out behind him like something crawling up his leg or caught on his shoe. She took him into the coatroom and Max watched the record spinning noiselessly in the machine while the nun knelt before him and rewound the cotton strip around his leg.

He continued to take dancing lessons into high school. The fact that he had talent obscured larger, sexist considerations: out of fifty or sixty students in the studio, only three were boys. For this reason he was in great demand at the yearly recitals, held each June at Indian River High. The three boys ran on and offstage like overworked vaudevillians. During the school year they performed an abbreviation of the recital—the cream of the revue—once or twice a month. He and the other two boys and a few girls would entertain at the Veterans' Home, the Kiwanis or a remote nursing home. For these performances Miss Weeks received seventy-five dollars, of which she gave twenty to the piano player. The children got the experience. Members of the audience were apt to get up and dance with you. Marie insisted only that Max be picked up and brought home each time.

It seemed entirely possible to him that, if he liked, he could be a professional dancer. Word of this idea may have got out, either directly through something he said or from the enthusiasm he brought to performing. His idea was to go to New York and become a gypsy, a chorus boy. This would lead to stardom on the musical stage. For a girl this was considered moderately respectable, if rare; it was called becoming a Rockette. Miss Weeks had been a Rockette. But for boys, at thirteen or fourteen, dancing lessons were only suspect.

Following his solo performance in his last recital at the end of his fifteenth year, he was informed by Penny, who wore an expression of wide-eyed naïveté, that John was afraid dancing would make his son a fairy—a remark that had been addressed to Marie. This accounted for the charged silence and polite applause greeting his somewhat arty routine. Miss Weeks had wanted to try something different; a balletic element had been added in certain steps which, even as he performed them, he recognized as effeminate. Out it went over the footlights, a message that John read clearly.

Max was meant to hear the fairy remark. That was the point. If it was supposed to be a shot across his bow it was poorly aimed, scoring instead a direct hit; the ship of dance went straight to the bottom, and with it the idea of Broadway. He quit taking lessons, and found they had been free for years. In the early, difficult years, when they had seemed a luxury, Marie had tried to stop them on financial grounds. But boys were so scarce Miss Weeks had been happy to teach him for nothing. And Marie could think of no other reason for him to stop.

They drove on certain Sundays to Brooklyn, to Avenue U and Avenue J, to John's and Marie's families. Max was distrustful of any force of organization that would choose a system of names out of the alphabet. Who could care for such streets? Everything was unintentionally close together, with abbreviations of driveways, compressed approximations of front yards, the houses nearly but not quite touching. His relatives, and the neighbors with whom their lives had become entwined, were exaggerated, theatrical and raw. The old people seemed fierce, especially in the eyes and around the mouth, with intensely held opinions and vivid personal quirks. John's mother, Grandma Desiderio, talked in the dialect of a Sicilian hill town, delivered with such high-pitched staccato urgency as to be unintelligible except in terms of stark dread and alarm. Her funeral was like an opera, the ripe, full-blown production of a transplanted culture reverting in death to the old, intense ways; with women in black sitting in vigil for three days like crows on a lawn, with huge floral tributes—a clock of carnations stopped horti-culturally at the hour of death, and her favorite chair fatly reproduced lifesize in mums and roses, with a macabre scene at the end when Grandpa Desiderio, momentarily roused from confusion by the enormity of his loss, the horror of change, broke loose from those supporting him, rushed down the chapel aisle and threw himself into his wife's coffin, sobbing one last time on the hardened flesh, calling her wretched names, hating her for leaving him behind.

For five or six years when Max was in grammar and then high school, Marie ran a dress shop in town with a woman neighbor. John wanted to get ahead. He wanted his own company. The shop would help to make that possible and it prospered in a small way. Marie filled the racks with clothes she herself would wear. The Rosary Society women came and returned because Marie told them what looked good and what didn't. Her prices were fair, her taste highly developed for a small town. She planted evergreen bushes and seasonal flowers in boxes across the front. One Halloween the picture Max painted on their window won a prize.

Marie's partner, who lived across the street, had two sons, the elder of whom, though two years younger than Max, was his closest friend. The boy was named Donny but called Dee. Dee was honey-colored and blond, a Ganymede. They had grown up together, their friendship reinforced by that of their mothers, but when Max was fifteen it was suggested that Dee was too young for him, and Max was encouraged to play with his other friends, particularly Scott. He saw Dee less often. But when he did, Max was seized by an overpowering desire to touch him, an impulse he half understood and disguised. Dee complained that Max jumped on him every time they met, and thereafter Max held himself back, feigning a composure and indifference that left him exhausted and confused.

When he was fifteen he played spin-the-bottle at a small private party, with a wheel of eight or ten girls and boys; everyone. The bottle spun for so long it seemed to have the capacity to choose. He remembered, also, eating up one end of a wax straw and thinking that if it were a strand of spaghetti it would need another five minutes. Sharon Woolf gave him a kiss at the middle, just her lips around the straw, she perhaps having eaten a bit more of it than he.

Max's brother Jack was oddly protective, making his friends behave with Max as they would with his sisters, shutting them up every time some wisp of innuendo escaped them. Dee and his other friends seemed to have had similar educators, protectors, censors. But one night in a tent in Dee's back yard, the classic rites of masturbation occurred. The impossible tickle yielded a teaspoonful of liquid that had waited so long for tapping as to have turned lightly green, or so it seemed by candlelight.

Shortly afterward, a girl who cleaned for Marie once a week, named Louella, started to rearrange Max's bed on the last day of a dragged-out flu. Suddenly she pulled down the covers and his pajamas and put his penis in her mouth; then sat on him. She was about twenty. Max was dazed. When Louella did not return the following week and her name was never mentioned, he was sure they had been found out and she had been dismissed. But Louella had left town, planning her departure so well as to take all of her husband's furniture with her, leaving him only the bed. She had knocked off Max as a gesture of significance, marking the end of a period she had come to find squalid and boring.

He experienced some guilt momentarily. Louella was

black, older, in his mother's employ. But the taboos, fear of reprisal, or disease, lasted only as long as it took for the voluptuary in him to catalog the pleasures of the experience—the heat and silkiness, the scent, the excitement. It was Louella who showed him the power and directness of sex; Louella who took with her, besides Max's cherry, one of his horse figurines, as a memento of the affair—the one he had thrown away and retrieved—and which he only missed later.

That same summer he found his uncle Dan's war souvenirs in the attic, in a dusty untouched box marked Private and shoved deep under the eave. It contained two German lugers and a small black pistol—all unloaded; folded flags, a black saucepot helmet with a silver spike in the top, swastika armbands and odds and ends; also Vargas calendars and girlie books that filled Max with excitement, not for the pictures so much as for the palpable, twenty-years-gone passion they had evoked in his soldier-uncle.

He brought his friend Scott up to the attic to show him the find. Together, rummaging further, they found another carton under the eave. This contained an empty bombshell of brass, letters, pictures—one of himself as a baby and with the inscription *My pet* on the back in his aunt Phoebe's hand—and a Purple Heart, in a purple box lined with ivory silk.

A Purple Heart, Scott said. This was a serious soldier.

Also more pinups and a gynecology textbook that fell open to certain pages. The attic was not insulated. It was early summer. The sweat broke out on their brows, under their arms. Down at the bottom of the carton were two yellowed German magazines and another in English that they took out to a cooler part of the attic, near the oxeye in the gable. They lay down on a double mattress on the floor to read them. It seemed expedient, halfway through, to wrestle. Over the pretext of turning a page or rereading a passage, Scott pushed him aside. Max pushed him back. They needed to manifest this new sensation immediately, force against force. Scott pinned him, but in such a way as to underscore his dominance. Max was held captive. Scott scissored his legs around Max, lying along his side, their faces almost touching. One deft wrestler's trick and Scott had a free hand. With it he undid Max's belt, pulled his pants down around his knees, jerked him off. Max struggled throughout. That was how it was done. Afterward he felt weak. He thought, This weakens me, strengthens him.

On another occasion, the wrestling was more cursory, not because Max didn't try but because the outcome was certain. This time Scott came as well, holding it in his foreskin until he could stand up. Then making a quick turn of his hips, he released himself, and with a sound like a knock at the door, his semen hit the hollow attic wall.

🌳

In certain years several big storms came in the same season, before the leaves fell and after the sun had faded down. Six willows in the park were blown down one year in a gale that followed three days of rain. This was the storm that took the big oak in back, an ash on the side by the fence and two of the lindens in front. A brand-new 1952 Buick Roadmaster was in the garage. The oak, which was very old and eight or ten feet around, swayed back and forth, toward them then away, as they watched at the windows waiting for it to topple. It was mid-afternoon and storm dark, with brilliant white flashes of lightning and huge surprise cracks of thunder that made Max's neck sink down in his shoulders. The earth at the base of the tree split and heaved. Either the house or the garage and car would get it because the tree rocked on a single axis between them. The ash went, meanwhile, with first a crack as if it had snapped in half, then a long falling swish down to a thump that rocked the house and flattened the fence. Max watched from his window with openmouthed wonder, there being no difference in the spectacle before him than if it had extended to the whole world. When the lights went, it added a new dimension to the terror, as if the storm had somehow got into the house.

It was the garage that took the big oak finally, if not completely. At the property line another oak, nearly as large, caught it as it fell, sparing the new Buick and the next house beyond. It was in all the county papers as an arboreal miracle. From the next day on a heavy smell of earth and resin filled the yard. He climbed up on the oak trunk as if onto the back of a huge dead thing fallen from the sky. The man from the insurance company walked around shaking his head, disavowing any responsibility. They would fix the garage, which was insured, but not remove the tree. It was the first time Max heard the expression, Act of God, as if God, at least for these moments, had accounted for His whereabouts.

Fine, John said, you fix the roof first and then I'll remove the tree, and clapped his hands together once.

It took weeks for it to be cleared away. A large crater in the lawn between the house and the garage marked where the oak had stood. Talk of digging it out and putting in a swimming pool came to nothing. A piece of the tree trunk, which was cut and lowered in sections by rope, fell sixty feet and crushed their swing, looping the crossbar down to the ground so that a large M was formed. The swing was not replaced. It seemed that that part of their lives was over.

In that same year—1952—John lost his job. Life was apparently too complicated for a mild little liver tonic and the company went bankrupt. Then Grandpa and Grandma Defilippo died, Danilo of stomach cancer and Angela not long afterward of congestive drowning after heart failure. Max saw her coffin lurch up onto the pall-bearers' shoulders in a way that must, he thought, have moved the body inside. Sometime after that Marie miscarried in an early month of her fifth pregnancy and went into menopause, a fact Max didn't learn until he was past thirty. He discovered his mother one afternoon sitting in her room, her faced flushed, with a tired, pleading expression in her eyes. He asked her what was wrong and she said, I guess I miss my mother, darling. But her mother had been dead for many years. Then she said, After I had Penny I lost a baby. I was just thinking who it might have been.

Apparently they lived for a time on what the dress shop brought in, which wasn't much when divided between the two families. John began several projects at home. One provided people with diagrams for the landscaping of their new suburban homes, for the construction of which, usually, the ground had been strip-mined. This was an idea that came with a short correspondence course. Using clear plastic forms, he drew pencil designs of shrubs and treetops, like stylized blossoms; these he placed, in various orders and sizes, around the drawn foundations of his clients' split-level houses. Another project was the development and production in the basement of a rust-proof paint, which he called Jemm, after the first initials of himself, Marie, and Dee's parents,

Ellen and Myron. Perhaps some of the profits from the dress shop, which they jointly owned, were put into the Jemm idea. They sat around the dining room table on Sundays after Mass; John ran the meeting and they went over the books, usually but not always without incident.

Weekdays the house was empty when Max got home. One afternoon he came in and found Penny lurking halfway up the stairs, where the banister joined the ceiling in a V. Her hair was flaming orange. Help me she said. Max pedaled his bike to Calloway's to buy the antidote color. No one noticed at dinner. On a similar afternoon she taught him how to smoke cigarettes. It startled him to realize that she, whom he had so protected, learned such things before he did.

In 1956, rather in the nature of a breakthrough, and just as Robin was going off to college, John was hired as assistant production manager for a national cosmetics company. His salary was eighteen thousand dollars a year—a fortune. Within a year he was made manager of the eastern division. He worked long hours and was irritable at dinner. Max remembers his mother looking up the table, slapping down a spoon and saying, John, would your face crack if you smiled? Another time, they opened their napkins and each found a hundred dollar bill inside, which, however, they did not get to keep. The lesson involved was purely visual. John bought a long black Cadillac, which the neighbors came over to touch. Jack went from college to law school. In 1958 John was made vice-president in charge of eastern production, at twenty-four thousand a year. He worked sixteen-hour days, was seldom seen, hated his boss and developed an ulcer.

John had done it only for the money and now he saw that he had enough. The dress shop was sold and with this, his savings and money raised among the Desiderios in exchange for shares, John quit his job and bought a small bankrupt paint company in Passaic. They called the company Jemm Products. Within six months of his resignation, the cosmetics company asked him to return at his own price. Allegedly, their production was off 17 percent. John was gratified by the decline, but refused.

Jemm did moderately well from the first but in 1959 Jack was in his last year at law school and both Robin and Max were in college—Robin as a senior and Max as a freshman. The next year Jack was finished but now Penny, having declined the idea of college, went off to a kind of secretarial-finishing school that specialized in the production of air hostesses, and was even more expensive than Robin's smart Catholic college in Philadelphia. Penny took courses in Makeup and Carriage, and the Preparation of Short Meals.

In high school Max had had two or three major girl friends, of the type and class that precluded sex until just after or perhaps before the prom. The senior prom was like a mock mass wedding. His friend Scott, with whose body he had wrestled in the attic, was the king of the prom. Subsequently he married the queen, by whom he had four children and was never heard from again. It was Scott who showed Max how a human teenager was supposed to behave, which is to say the actions if not the precise feelings. These remained beyond Max. He had sex with no one but himself, in the afternoons when Marie was at the dress shop, his father at work and Penny at cheerleading practice. Looking out the window of his room, his rocklike penis in his hand, he watched members of the track team jog by on their way to the park. Once he brought his girl friend Milly home with him. They had petted heavily on countless dates, kissed passionately; he had even put his hand inside her moist panties and fingered her. The problem was that she was too tight to fuck. They had already tried twice and she confessed to having tried once with another boy. The visit to Max's house was planned to correct this condition in a more leisurely fashion than was possible in the car. The expression Max later learned for what happened was— like stuffing an oyster into a parking meter. Milly subsequently confided she later was surgically stretched by the family doctor, a procedure Max imagined as requiring expanding plugs and screws. But at the time he took it all on himself.

He did not then attempt sex with another creature until the summer of his junior year in college, 1962, in Munich. John had offered them each a car or a trip and he took the trip, thinking, correctly, that he would get the car too. Alone in Paris, in a madras jacket and a blue beret, he happened to witness a street crime and to be interviewed on camera. In Munich a few days later he saw the newsreel in a theater at the train station—with the beret, the appallingly familiar face, a French narration. He missed the train and waited for the short program to run through again. As the audience underwent a number of changes he noticed that certain men got up to leave and then sat down or stood in other places. It was this fact as much as seeing himself on screen that made him want to miss his train and stay. His face, made slightly ovoid by the fisheye lens, had just reappeared when a man in a dark suit and tie sat down beside him and pressed a leg against his.

C'est vous là, n'est-ce pas? the man said.

Max nodded. The man's hand slid over and helped itself to a souvenir grope, to which Max acquiesced as if reluctantly giving an autograph. They had coffee together in the station, then went to a hotel nearby. The man held him close under the eiderdown. They did not actually have sex beyond frottage. Early in the morning a woman knocked loudly at the door, ranting in German. Amazingly, she used a passkey and came in, spitting like Mania rrom every balustrade. After an incomprehensible diatribe against the man, she turned and said something vile to Max in German. He replied, in Italian, that he did not speak German, at which instant the woman adjusted her language dial to Italian for a vicious and fluent string of insults and abuse; he was a *troia*—something like a slut—and perverted slime. Her nostrils flared and tilted upward in an attitude of fierce indignation and revulsion.

They dressed and fled. When they came out of the hotel the man went one way and Max returned to the station, harried, fleeing the crime, boarding the next train, for the next stop on his tour.

It had been clear to him since high school that all directions toward intimacy with men were strictly policed—all the mis- or half-understood expressions, gestures, symbols and rituals that represented sex and that, if pursued at length, might lead to it. For Max this meant the existence of a line down the middle of all his connections with men, a point beyond which it was forbidden, or at least dangerous, to go. For a long time it was possible to imagine this line as being rather far to the left of convention. He could pretend that everyone understood and appreciated the allure of men but chose not to respond to it for proscribed cultural reasons, just as he did. It was clear also that he had no choice in the matter other than the repression or manifestation of these desires, for they came unbidden; they could not be changed or altered, only repressed or disguised.

It was in this mood of slightly paranoid circumspection that he passed his college years. By 1963, when he graduated, Jemm had moved quarters twice, changed its name to Mara Products, using John's nickname for Marie, and lost two partners—Myron and Ellen—to the vicissitudes of business and friendship. The Desirs were by now nearly rich. The expensive years of college and weddings were behind them; everyone but Max was married and living elsewhere. First the house in Indian River was lavishly redecorated. Then they bought a second house at the beach, then a forty-foot fishing boat, also called the *Mara*. John joined the Naval Cadets, a national boat-owners' association that organized private cruises to Mystic and Newport and Lake Champlain. Every winter they went to the Caribbean on the *Oceanic*, John with three tuxedos and Marie with ten or twelve long gowns. Marie received jewelry and furs on her birthdays, Christmas and anniversaries. One Christmas, during the Vietnam War, they started opening gifts at nine in the morning and didn't finish until after dark.

The day after his graduation from college Max returned to Italy, to Florence, which he had seen the summer before, entering the city as if on the trail of closely interpreted clues left for him by something outside himself. He had come to write but arrived to find he had nothing to write about, that his ideas and experiences were banal and frivolous—frivolous in the wrong way. Each night, too warm and too exhilarated to sleep, he took walks through the narrow, benign, empty streets. Having done this twice, it became a ritual. Emerging into the Piazza della Signoria was like slipping onstage. Any number of operatic moments; as beside him, livid blood from the severed head of Cellini's Perseus dripped on the marble bench. He made the connection between dissatisfaction over his writing attempts and the quality of his experience. He felt he had done everything wrong thus far and must start over. He had put himself in the wrong places, learned the wrong attitudes—about himself, so that he didn't know who he was; about his education, so that he hadn't learned anything; and about sex. At twenty-two, except for Louella, and in odd incomplete ways Milly, Scott, and Dee, he was still a virgin.

On these night walks a number of men regularly presented themselves to him. One in particular was apt at any moment to appear upstage or over by the fountain, always at a discreet but interested distance. He seldom followed Max; however, Florence *centrostorico* was small enough to account for frequent and seemingly coincidental encounters. It was this person's genius to play young tourists like piccolos. He waited and watched and when Max got up and came across the piazza to speak, he was not particularly surprised.

They became friends of a strange kind, the kind that sleep together, not as an invention of their own but as a matter of local custom. That was how one met and expanded one's circle in Florence. The man took him to a house just outside the city, where eight or ten of his friends had assembled after dinner, as they did every night somewhere or other. It was usual for someone to leave, pick up whomever he pleased, and return to liven the party; a little dancing, perhaps a striptease. The house was quiet and perfectly dark. Inside, several tall rooms had been lighted only with candles; five or six couples danced to soft music. It was not the senior prom. After introducing Max to the others, the man asked him to dance. Slowly, in little swaying steps, they turned, always counterclockwise, making one full revolution before Max realized they had been left alone, each of the couples having slipped out of the room behind his back. Another full revolution to demonstrate, politely, that they needn't rush, then a kiss put them into a spiral that landed them on a pile of cushions on the floor, in a position of incipient coitus. It was not, he realized, an act that one did; it was something that occurred. He lowered himself onto and somehow into the man in the same extended motion, in a way that then and ever after he thought of as miraculously easy and comfortable. The immediate senses were flooded to the extent that he failed to notice faces watching from the shadows, from around corners, behind the curtains, through the door.

Coming home along the river afterward, he had the impression of stepping out of himself, as from behind a wall through which he had peered as through the false eyes of a portrait. Later, when told he had been observed, his embarrassment was mitigated by compliments and flattery, plus the feeling of having given and received erotic pleasure, somewhat alleviating the cheapness implied. Never mind; they spied on everyone sooner or later. It was a comfort to him, which they would never have guessed, to have at last done something worth watching.

He allowed himself then to surrender to a limitless fascination for men. He learned the circuit quickly. It was not extensive: the places, habits, streets, faces, hours, ways. He was shown a lot of it and discovered the rest on his own, chancing upon Lilo, who in this case was a conductor on the number four bus to San Marco. Lilo drove a scooter, looked good in slacks, had two separate and antithetical lives, one with a wife and baby, another with the circle into which Max had been introduced.

This circle was tangential to a higher, more exalted set of homosexuals who emerged from and disappeared into the gardens of the aristocracy in the hills toward Pisa; stories of life at court in exchange for sex and street gossip—the titled queens and the working class. They bought Max clothes, took him to the opera and dinners, to museums in the afternoons and coffee at Doney's in Piazza Republica at a certain hour. Lilo, not a thug but not a queen, picked him up in the morning on his motor scooter and took him to Fiesole for the view and coffee, or to San Miniatello to sit on the cool stones. They did not have sex for nearly a month, due to the complexity of Lilo's existence and Max's unwillingness to bring him back to the pensione, which was forbidden.

Having shown such patience and respectful forbearance, it was doubly shocking then that Lilo, when he got the chance, raped Max, or at least committed rape on a body willing to be raped. It was painful, unnecessary and bestial, negating all the romantic looks and charged intimacy, replacing them with anger, shock, hurt. It was, if Max had wanted to experience something a little different, the exact reenactment of one hundred million wedding nights—the rape of the beloved bride. He might even say he now knew what the Sabines felt.

After Lilo, Max became friendly with the only other proletarian in the circle, a waiter whose parents owned a restaurant in Prati. Max was not attracted to the ones with manners and rich families—effeminate complications absent in the working class. The queens spoke to him in English, each move they made delicately telegraphed for approval. With Lilo and the waiter anything was likely to happen, suddenly and to great effect. The excitement came in their directness.

In the midst of these romantic friendships he was, perhaps by way of subjective compensation, atrociously unfaithful with strangers from the streets, the park; quite the little whore. He allowed nothing to hold him back, except perhaps an unwillingness to miss or be late for meals at the pensione. The imposition of a secret, vast and unorthodox sex life upon an Edwardian schedule gave him a vivid sense of being, and an absorbed interest in the goings-on that he had never before known. Any impulse to flee the palace in search of men was a command, no matter what the hour. Soundlessly he would slip along the dark halls to the door and down the hundred steps, drawn to the streets like an addict, or like some small and simple animal who has only to reach out, within a garden of abundance, to take what is required; an addiction constantly appeased, constantly growing.

In September, by prearrangement, John and Marie arrived to collect him for a trip to Messina, their first, to visit the Defilippos. Having seen only photographs of Marie, the family pronounced her indeed the double of Barbara Stanwyck. Concetta, Marie's aunt, who had survived the earthquake of 1908 and her two sisters, had shrunk to the size of a child.

Do you remember anything? the tiny woman asked, holding Marie's hand.

It was fifty years ago, *Nonna,* Marie replied.

I will tell you all, my dear, Concetta said. All. Your dear father, your dear mother and her need to be with him. She told you nothing about it?

Yes, *Nonna,* she told me, but it was so long ago. Marie picked up her wineglass, into which the old woman had put three or four peach slices covered with wine.

No, *joia,* wait, wait, Concetta said in her screechy little voice. I'll tell you when the moment comes.

Concettina, who never went out of the house, took them personally to the mausoleum, to see the crypts of her mother—Marie's grandmother—and of the baby, Victoria, Marie's sister, who had died in infancy. The mummy had entered a new phase. Cobwebs thickened with dust had fossilized into beaded strings that caught the light, like spun glass. It was apparent now that the lips and eyelids had been sewn closed.

My mother, Concettina screeched in the gloom. *La bella madre!* Come look. Isn't she beautiful?

Marie had taken Max's hand and stood slightly behind John's arm, a corner around which she made an effort to hide. She said softly, Oh my God.

Concetta, turning to Marie, said, That's your grandmother, my dear . . . Can you imagine?

They stayed in Messina four days, visiting with everyone, looking over the old photographs and letters, auditioning family and friends. They were brought around to the factories, the warehouses, the farm, the villa, down the coast to Catania where there was more, and to Taormina for the view. Since the war the Defilippos also sold appliances and light fixtures. John placed an order for two of their largest crystal chandeliers and numerous other fixtures for the new house being built in Hillcrest, which was considered correct and thoughtful, and for which John got everything at half-price.

Along the sea road, Marie asked the driver to stop. She remembered this spot, where her mother fished. They got out and she went down to the water's edge to a spit of rocks. She said, pointing a few feet away, I stood right there with my mother. Marie looked out across the straits, then at the little beach, the houses, the hills and trees behind.

She fished the morning we left, Marie said. Right here where we're standing. Some big fish, I can tell you. If she hadn't fished we wouldn't have left and you would never have been born, Max. Can you see how a little thing like that can make a big difference?

He said goodbye to them in Rome, from whence they flew to Paris and he returned to Florence with permission to remain another six months. Arriving after midnight, he left his bags at the train station. Ravenous, wired and vibrating with anticipation, his mind flooded with the images of rampant organs and melting eyes, he roamed the darkened streets and alleys like a soundless, gliding shark pursuing the sonics of hunger.

In the *Cascine*, the large park along the western reach of the Arno at one end of the city, he was arrested by a plainclothesman whose passivity Max had misinterpreted. He spent the night in an Army blanket on a cement shelf in the police station by the Duomo. He was questioned twice. Did he know that the act he had been caught committing—either they did not have a word for this act or its utterance was forbidden—was a crime against nature and the laws of God? He denied committing a crime. He was a tourist out walking, lost in the interstices of refined aesthetics, in the appreciation of Florence and all its amber angles as a work of art.

In the morning he was given sweet black coffee, was fingerprinted and photographed, and then, without having seen a lawyer or magistrate, was put into a Black Maria and driven upriver to a huge old prison outside Arezzo, called *La Stella Nera*. He was put in a cell by himself and given a plate of pasta, a raw egg and a *panino*. He wondered what he was supposed to do with a raw egg. The guards, through the grate, would not answer his questions or tell him the time; no matter what he asked they would say, Yes, soon; it would be soon.

No one knew he was there. He would not be reported missing at the pensione because he had not actually returned. His bags were checked at the train station. His parents were gone. He waited. On the third morning, three raw eggs later, he was led out of one wing of the prison, through an enormous rotunda and into another wing, into a small interior room in which a man asked statistical questions and typed the responses. Then he was taken into another room in which a man sat calmly behind a bare desk. Max demanded to know why he had been held incommunicado for three days. He was an American citizen. He had committed no crime.

It was a crime to do what was done in the *Cascine*, the man said. Everyone was held incommunicado until they had seen the magistrate—him. The delay was unfortunate, due to a backlog in the system.

After this interview Max was transferred to a different wing and put in a cell with two Italians. He presented the three eggs as a house gift, which the older, quieter cellmate accepted and cooked over a hotplate in the corner, giving them back to Max fried, with a fork and napkin and a side of prosciutto and cheese. The other cellmate was younger than Max, no more than seventeen. He had been caught stealing a car, his third offense. He did not think he would get more than five years. The older man, the cook, had been awaiting trial, also for auto theft, for three months, considered a typical delay. His name was Enzo and this was his cell, run according to his rules and extensive arrangements. After a few hours the younger thief popped up onto Max's bunk offering a cigarette. They talked while Enzo cooked dinner in the corner, passing them the results on white china restaurant plates. When Max asked why Enzo was being so kind, the boy whispered that Enzo thought Max—here called Massimo—was probably a personage and would help them when he was released.

This was reassuring only until he realized it didn't mean anything, lying through the night on the top shelf as if filed away and forgotten; wondering if he would ever be freed, if like Enzo he would have to wait months for his trial. He wondered what he didn't and couldn't know about his arrest, the law, the missing pieces, the facts as the police knew them. Was the commissioner or the warden or the magistrate a fiend in these matters? Later he realized it must all have come from the plainclothesman who had arrested him. This act Max interpreted as a treacherous betrayal—given that they had already begun to have sex when the man drew back and changed into an arresting officer of the state. Several times during the hours at the police station others suggested he simply be let go. But the man had refused. Deliberately Max was fed into the system, step by procedural step, until a part of him, like a part of his clothing, his shirttail or cuff, was properly hooked and ratcheted and pulled into the vast machine.

The next day was shower day. Their cell's turn came in the afternoon. Enzo provided him with soap. It was in the showers that Max first saw Nick. He was taller, bigger, finer than everyone else in the room, in such a way as to seem better fed, on superior food, fresh milk and meat and garden fruit—an American college boy. They stopped washing and stared at each other, like two statues that mark the entrance to something fabulous.

Afterward, fifty or so men at a time were allowed to stand outside for an hour in the yard. Nick came up to him.

What's your name? he asked in English, smiling.

Max Desir.

I'm Nick Flynn. What are you in for?

I was picked up in the park, Max replied. And you?

Dope, I'm afraid. My apartment, not me. I was arrested at the airport coming back. No one's guilty in here of course. My apartment did it, Your Honor. He laughed.

Max put his hand on Nick's arm. Can you tell me what to do? I'm in a cell with two car thieves.

Do you know anyone in Florence? Max shook his head and Nick said, Well, I do. Have you got a lawyer? If you don't nominate a good one they give you a turkey and stamp you through. You must imagine, he said, that you are dealing with Napoleon, because things haven't changed since then.

Have you been here long? Max asked.

A few weeks. The person who can help me is out of town. He named a sister of the President of Italy. Max was dazzled.

She's due back this week. You are to picture the Emperor's daughter-in-law. One word from her and I could spring a whole wing of the Black Star.

Why does it have such a sinister name? he asked.

You haven't seen it from the outside. It's got five wings like a star and a black roof.

And the sex I've been hearing about? Max said.

A crackdown a few days ago in Torino. It's worse than any park in here. Be careful. Trust no one. He smiled again.

A bell rang. They took each other's hand. I'll see you later, Nick said. Nominate Bandini as your lawyer. Two thousand bucks.

Later, after dinner chez Enzo, a note was handed up to Max in his bunk. On the outside was written in Italian: *For the American in D-Wing with the long hair.* Inside, in English, it said:

> Max, we can get each other out. Tell Bandini to call Firenze 055.889 and to speak only to you-know-who. Don't let anyone hear you say the name. Say I'm here. Nick Flynn. And that it's the apartment, not me. She'll do the rest. Sweet Dreams. Nick.

In the corner at the bottom he had drawn a tiny heart.

Max's announcement nominating Bandini as his lawyer only confirmed Enzo's instinctive opinion, which itself had been greatly enhanced by the arrival of the note, that Max would soon be free and therefore able to help from the outside. For the next several days he produced constant and prodigious meals from nowhere. In their interview, Max gave the lawyer the telephone number of the sister of the President of Italy and the rest happened very quickly. Max was brought into a visitors' room. Bandini, a dapper little man of about sixty with beautiful white hair and a cane, spoke habitually in a whisper.

She is coming! he hissed. Here! Her Excellency! No trial, no formalities, *niente!* This, Signore Massimo, is true power—bald, bold and limitless! It is difficult to imagine that the signorino should be so favorably connected. . . . The Virgin herself, meaning no disrespect, could not have done this more quickly, with such sure, masterful strokes. . . . It is known, he whispered even more confidentially, that her brother would sooner die than cross her. How is it, if one may ask that—

Bandini was interrupted here by the arrival of the lady herself, heavily veiled, dressed completely in black, not an inch of skin showing anywhere. She ignored Bandini and extended a gloved hand to Max.

How do you do? she said in faultless English. Would you mind leaving just as you are? It would be simpler.

What about Nick? Max asked.

He insists on getting his things. Thus the delay. My dear, perhaps after this experience you will have some idea of how stupid these Italians are. I apologize for the entire country . . . They are all pigs.

She turned to Bandini. Signore, thank you for coming. It is most kind.

Signor Bandini appeared to be inspecting the lady's shoes. Anything, Signora, at any time, in any way.

Would you please now take Signor Desir to my car? She handed him a paper. It's signed by the warden and should see you through. She turned back to Max.

❦ ─────────────────────────────────────

They have my passport, wristwatch and keys, he said.

Oh no they don't, the little bastards. She extracted a manila envelope from a black satchel he had not even noticed, and handed it to him.

You will learn, she said, if you are to be Nicky's friend, that Lydia—here she partially lifted her veil, exposing a pretty, middle-aged face, blue eyes and a pleasant, mischievous smile—overlooks nothing. *A presto*, she said, and disappeared in a waft of veils through the doorway.

Bandini was muttering. He took out a handkerchief and mopped his forehead.

What about the trial? Max said.

She has had the whole thing erased! the lawyer replied. That's the point! Erased! As if it never happened! You were not here. You *are* not here! He took out a pair of spectacles and examined the paper Lydia had given him. *Dio, Dio*, he whispered to himself.

They were now on their way across the floor of the rotunda, moving toward an enormous door that looked from the inside like the entrance to a cathedral.

What about the people who arrested me?

The police? If there is any trouble, even a whisper, Bandini whispered, they too will be removed. He stopped, his hand on Max's arm, and inquired, having suddenly thought of it, Does the signore require revenge? If so, I would think that a word in the signora's private ear . . .

The car was not at the entrance. Bandini said something imperious to the guard, who picked up a phone in a toy soldier's striped booth beside the door.

Some minutes passed, with Max on the edge of sharp, tumbling emotions, as if he had been drugged; the keenest, relief, was mixed with a sense of excitement at seeing and being with Nick again. Waiting for him on the prison steps Max imagined him: the tall, pale, chunky body of a wrestler of the 169-pound class—the image from the showers; a pair of calm, dark, round, nearly bovine eyes set over small features—Nick's face in the yard.

A small but expensive black car with black windows glided through an archway and drew up to the bottom of the steps. A chauffeur opened the rear door. Nick leaned out.

Max! he said, laughing. Let's go before they change their fucking minds.

With a wave to Bandini, who had turned to stone, Max rushed down the steps and got into the car. As they were moving away, down the long gravel drive, Lydia threw back her veils and began removing her gloves. Nick took Max's hand, and Lydia said, Darlings, isn't this great fun!

After picking up Max's bags at the station, they drove down the valley toward Pisa, entering a small town and then a pair of gates in a wall of its main square, after which the car climbed a steep hill at such an angle that the road in front of them fell from view. They came out at the top within a fortress, built on an outcropping of rock in the middle of the town, like an acropolis. The top of it was not more than an acre across, on several levels. At its center, rising out of a villa constructed around its base, rose a square stone tower two hundred feet tall, topped with a loggia that commanded the countryside for miles in every direction. Up the valley in the distance one could see the mist like dust over Florence.

No one will disturb you here, Lydia said, not getting out of the car. Nick, you know the way around. The place is yours until you've quite . . . recovered. Really, I'm so ashamed. You must both try to forget. I'll call you from

Florence. Max, such a pleasure. She held out her hand. I will be back in a few days and we'll have a long, long talk. In the meantime, enjoy, my darlings. From now on you must take care of each other ... Lydia can't be everywhere. She blew them a kiss and the car was gone down the side of the hill.

They spent a week in the tower, the first three days in the principal bedroom and bath, sending down for food as if in a hotel. The single, continuous act of making love, with extensive permutations, was hours, even days long, and resembled a kind of struggle on the part of each of them to get somehow within the confines, the borders, the barriers of each other's body. Lying beside Nick while he slept, watching the satiny back rise and fall, and the eyelids tremble in a dream, Max said, I love you, to the sleeping figure.

IV

It seemed a change of venue was needed now that they were going to be a pair, and at Lydia's suggestion and with her help in finding an apartment, they moved to Rome, into a *superattico* near Piazza Navona. To the antiquarian on the ground floor and the local shopkeepers they were brothers, or at least cousins, but likely, as foreigners, to be anything at all. Lydia, with her extravagant costumes and veils, her mute chauffeur, fooled no one. The glint of adoration in everyone's eye when Max and Nick saw her to her car suddenly burst into a flame of respect that soon engulfed the neighborhood. Any official connection might have set them apart; that they should know the sister of the President marked them as *pezzi grossi*. In the market they were addressed as doctor and professor. The antiquarian, seizing a small opportunity, inquired if they had all the furniture they needed for their new apartment.

It was a grand little place with balconies off every

room, totally empty. They refused Lydia's offer to swing a few things through the window by crane, the staircase being too narrow for her idea of furniture. Instead they went to the flea market at Porta Portese, Lydia dressed as an English lady and speaking Italian like Ruth Draper. Gorgeous junk accumulated in their wake; when assembled, these objects gave the apartment a religious air, as in the public rooms of a convent, or the sitting room of a priest. Green lacquer walls, extricated grudgingly from the Italian house painter, threw every odd, aged piece into crisp relief—the candlesticks filched from country churches, a marble dog, a one-eyed St Agnes, hands clasped miserably before her as if in desperation over her missing eye. A couturier friend of Lydia's who was redoing his studio sent over fifty or sixty varicolored silk cushions no longer needed. This bright pile, in Max's fantasy, might better have been spread upon blazing desert sands beside a passing caravan. Out of the silent, attenuated riot of camels and cloth steps Nick, the dark herdsman. The hot sun through the open windows strikes their backs, the old furniture like bark beside their smooth young skin. Except for food or Lydia's arrangements, they might never have gone out.

His parents' letters from home shrieked with silent alarm. Moved to Rome! Might stay indefinitely! His father took the unusual step of writing to Max directly. Was this the moment to push the bird from the nest? Mr Desir, larger bird, even threatened to fly over personally if not told immediately what was going on.

So tell him, Nick said. Call him up. Write him a letter. You're with me now.

Impossible to call, only slightly less difficult to put into words, they worked on the reply message together, as they now did everything together. They mentioned *La Stella Nera*, Lydia's help, their intention to stay together always. John received the letter like a cannonball catcher on an off night—not without temporary damage to the midsection. He missed the niceties, the attempts at gentleness, the wish to be accepted, grasping only the headlines of the situation: *Son Gay, Father Distraught.*

Mr Desir wrote back that he should never have allowed Max to go to Florence in the first place. This had been the basic mistake for which he took all the blame. But to be homosexual was one thing; to be an expatriate was quite another, although perhaps in an unsavory way they were linked after all. In any event, when was he, when were *they,* coming home?

Oh not for years, darling, Lydia exclaimed when told the facts. Home to what? she demanded; to the ideas and sentiments of Queen Victoria? Let them work it out on their own for a while, in the abstract. You can't rush this sort of thing with Americans.

John wrote, No matter what, you're my son, and Max's allowance continued to arrive each month at the Banco di Roma.

Nick began an acting career with interviews with several Italian directors—set up of course by Lydia. He got extra work immediately, which led to small parts and actual scenes. His good looks were smoothed out by the camera into idealized perfection. You wondered about the director's taste and priorities in letting such a face flash by without lingering; or so Max thought, turning to Nick in the darkened theater with a smile, luxuriating in the mercury profile of his own film star. On occasion in the days of *Cinecittà,* a studio car would come for him early in the morning. If it were Marilyn Monroe getting into a limousine at five in the morning, Nick said, she would be carrying a pillow and practically walking in her sleep.

A woman named Isabella cleaned the apartment

three times a week, a job that consisted mainly of chasing dust mice across the empty floors on drafts from the balcony doors, and of preparing something like eggplant parmigiana or soup for lunch. They sat down to a meal served by a maid in a dining room in their own home, in a place at any rate which they had made themselves, *bent* on inventing a reasonable replica of life either as they had lived it as children or seen it in movies or dreams.

They settled in. This meant ordering suits and buying engraved stationery at Pineider. Max wrote stories. Nick joined a theater company that put on plays in English.

From the railings of their several balconies, set into the mansard roof so as to cut the streets from view, they held each other by the waist and looked out over the rooftops, at the tower of this, the dome of that, at the complacent neutrality of Rome. In the street they were foreigners of consequence; up here they were naked athletes of love, sailing over everything.

Max had been infatuated before this but had never got beyond the first, unrequited, reeflike stages of love. The dynamics of falling in love—so stormy, humiliating, exhilarating and changeable—were now replaced with those of *being* in love, which brought a sense of calm, the image of smooth turquoise water and a pearl beach, a lagoon of ease. This process seemed to have happened on its own.

He was the first to fall. Thereafter he wove a web of sexual and emotional enticement, binding Nick to him in tiny exquisite ways. He angled, as if for a huge fish, the bait being completion, union, the glamour of like minds and bodies, the promise of ambition, the sweetness of constant satisfaction. Every few days Max asked Nick what he wanted, what he missed, regretted, lacked. Max said he would find it, invent it, create it; or if it offended, strip it from his act, like an ugly prop or costume. They must talk. They must identify themselves to each other. They must be clever about their love, avoiding the bone-littered snares and traps set out by a jealous world.

Nick at first did not like to speak of any point further than two weeks in the future. A few years in New York had made him leery of plans, and alert and sensitive to possessiveness. He did not like taking showers together because of the overload of information and sensation—two elements at once. The discovery that he was occasionally skittish, to the edge of paranoia, meant that, at one point, probably in the aforementioned New York, he had been frightened by something, never specified. This weakness was visible only now and then; to Max it meant Nick needed him. He saw it the way he sometimes noticed a tiny scar on Nick's scalp, when the wind blew his hair up in a particular way.

It helped, it seemed, to have met in a foreign country where it was obvious, as it might not even have been clear at home, that they were alone and on their own. Nothing else interested them particularly. Each was incredibly vivid to the other, each being the one point of focus in the other's frame, a focus occasionally replaced on their walks through the city by the details on a monument of antiquity. But only for a moment. Always their attention snapped back to the other's face, to the nape of the neck, the fascinating, specieslike autonomy of the beautiful hands, the sweet, level connection of the eyes.

Lilo in Florence had lied, to intense sexual effect: *Te amo. Ti voglio bene.* Nick was the first to say it in English, the first perhaps ever to feel that way about Max. Max thought at the time that loving might almost have been enough. But being loved in return swept him away completely, and for good. He thought it was as if someone had put a spell on him, that he must always love whoever should be the first to love him back.

Nick loved Lydia like a mother. They had met on the Florentine circuit—the same one Max had glimpsed—which tended to throw together Florence's most sophisticated residents and her best-looking tourists. Nick had gone higher and Lydia had come down a bit, and they adored each other. Nick said they had not slept together nor had they ever considered it. Lydia was his glamorous mother, he her gorgeous son. Had his parents not still been living, back in Iowa, she'd have adopted him legally. Lydia appealed not only to the boy but to the actor in Nick. Her life had been dramatic even in the days before her brother's administration. She gave Nick a wonderful part to play, the cherished of the rich and sophisticated. In return he gave her the constant reciprocation of a quick, sensitive mind and the glamour of his stunning looks.

For man or woman, you're the ideal mate, Max said.

Nick had come to Europe during the first wave of its rediscovery by American youth in the sixties. He had put himself through college in a leisurely way, that is, through six colleges in five states and Mexico, moving on at will, finishing in New York City with, in the end, a philosophy degree from CCNY. He had known of his attraction to and for men since the age of nine, in the days when a man could take you for a ride in his automobile, have sex, and not kill you. During and after the six colleges, he hitchhiked through most of the United States; and then, rather naturally, he moved on to Europe, keeping it simple, traveling like a tourist of the later, *second* wave of discovery—the backpackers and hitchhikers, those seekers-after-good on their long way to India and Nepal. Nick was in no particular hurry, took no particular direction. He appreciated the hospitality of local tricks. The idea that London, Paris, Munich, Hamburg had dealt evenly with young men like him for centuries inspired confidence. He had the feeling that if he wandered from place to place with an open mind and high expectations, important and lucky things would happen to him.

In Florence he was whisked off the street and into Lydia's presence. The combination of shyness, good looks and sophistication in a tourist charmed her. They became friends. She found him a job as secretary to an English novelist so that he could take an apartment and stay awhile. Nothing was permanent or needed to be.

Then the novelist fell for Nick and it was necessary to leave. Nick sublet his flat for six months and went to Paris. Meanwhile the tenant dealt drugs out of the apartment. When Nick reentered the country he was arrested—guilty by association. Two weeks later, in the dark forbidding arms of *La Stella Nera*, he met Max.

They hardly saw anyone but Lydia. They would not hear from her for several weeks, which meant she was in Florence or traveling; then abruptly, irresistibly, she would appear or telephone with The Plan. She strongly favored visits to the country villas of old friends, weekends requiring great logistical migrations of guests and matériel—special food, wine, props, costumes, additional servants, treats, surprises—all the tools of the grand hostess.

We leave Thursday evening by car for Cetona, she announced one Wednesday by phone.

But that's tomorrow night, Nick said.

Don't *say* you're busy or I'll die, Lydia sighed into the phone. You two are the key to the whole thing. None of them would bother to drag their poor tired bones to the country *yet again* except to see you, my two gorgeous boys. And Saturday will be fancy dress. I'm dressing Max as a sixteenth-century Italian prince, for which I am bringing along certain death-defying diamonds.

I'll tell him, Nick said. What am I to be?

An Attic shepherd, darling, stripped down to a few sable pelts and the glories God gave you. I've hired two sheep. If you don't come, I swear we'll eat them.

The sheep stood about, lamplike, where they were put. Lydia's preparations might even have included sheep sedatives. The weekend company included an elderly monsignor who was Lydia's closest friend and principal social beard; a chic, darkly serious lesbian couple; a middle-aged Florentine count who was the monsignor's long-time companion; two American teachers of art, also middle-aged, married and male; and Max and Nick.

Saturday evening's dinner was fancy dress. Nani, the count, appeared as a nun. This was taken as an amusing and considerate reference to his consort, Monsignor Alessio, who did not dress. The two art professors were simply and tastefully fitted out as European court ladies in evening gowns and tiaras, like elderly princesses. The two lesbians came of course as men, resembling those of the lounge-lizard sort—convincing but not completely reputable. Lydia said she was Maria José, wife of Umberto II, the last Queen of Italy; her dress was made of cloth-of-gold, her hair piled high and gilded. Max wore tights, a black velvet doublet, and long ropes of Lydia's diamonds. Nick, nearly naked with crook and sheep, was awarded the prize for most beautiful and apt.

Monsignor Alessio appeared at every function on Lydia's schedule of dubious social value or political implication. His rank, age, and nearly papal demeanor kept him beyond reproach and out of political reach; this in spite of an open fondness for boys. Monsignor Alessio loved angels as they appeared in the form of young boys, *s'intendiamo-ci*. Such a party as this would never have been possible in Lydia's life, or even in the lives of her servants, without the correct and reassuring presence of the monsignor.

According to Nick, this evening's gay theme was not the reflection of Lydia's sexual preference but the clever idea of a thoughtful and busy hostess, as on another occasion she might, in the same spirit, assemble eight or ten businessmen or a half-dozen chefs. Lydia believed that theme parties encouraged conversation. In another way, and because of her devotion to Nick, the assembly had been chosen to please him and his new friend. If in some vaguely startling way, there was something jejune about the evening, it was perhaps because the lesbians and the art professors seemed deeply disturbed by the way they were dressed. They had mustered enough sangfroid to cross-dress; not enough to go on with it in company.

The monsignor, who had just taken a sip of wine, now accidentally touched the stem of his glass to his plate with a crystal chime, inadvertently stopping conversation and drawing everyone's attention. Giving them all back a startled look, Monsignor Alessio then fell forward on the table. For a long moment the others wordlessly regarded his slumped figure and purplish face, which rested like a baked apple on his empty plate, the wine he had not completely swallowed dribbling like juice in a pink trickle from his lips. Presently, with a kind of spasm or convulsion, the priest, together with his dinner service, slid from the table and landed without breakage on the thickly carpeted floor. Nani screamed. He pushed over his chair and ran around the table to help his friend.

Get a doctor! Help him! he screamed, holding the priest's head in his nun's lap. He can't die, he cried after a moment. He can't! I couldn't!

The lesbians in tuxedos stepped in, calming Nani, taking the last few beats of Monsignor Alessio's pulse, and even going so far as to blow a few extra breaths into his wilting lungs; but it was clear after a few minutes that the man was dead.

It had been his heart, concerning which this was the last of several incidents, but it seemed at the time, to Nick and Max, to be *them*. What strains had they put on the old man's failing health? Not that they had ever spent a moment alone with him, or thought of it. But it was death at close range, the first for either of them. And it seemed, like so much in their lives—as for instance their meeting in prison—to have some larger meaning. This impression was further developed a few weeks later when the host of a similar weekend house party, at which Lydia was not a guest, just as suddenly dropped dead, this time not actually in their presence but very soon after leaving it.

I'm *swamped* with requests to get you for the weekend, Lydia announced.

That's not funny, Nick said.

Angeli del morte, they're calling you, she went on. Are you both already quite booked up?

It's appalling really, Nick said. We are thinking of leaving Rome.

Leaving Rome! Just because a few old people drop dead? You'll turn into nomads at that rate.

I have the possibility of work in New York, and Max's father has practically ordered him home.

Ahh, Lydia mused.

Or London, Nick said.

Darling, take a few weeks in Positano, to clear the head. London would only put you to sleep and I don't think Rome is done with you, somehow. . . .

But the part in New York did materialize and Mr Desir said Max would have to come back to the United

States or get a job. Feeling the way they did, they let the current carry them home.

At the airport and for the forty-minute drive home to Hillcrest, John registered a hard-edged and total silence, leaving Marie—half turned in her seat—to ask the questions and give the news. That no one else had been there to welcome them was deeply ominous.

When he got his mother alone for a moment, Max embraced her and solemnly apologized—not for himself and Nick but for the oddity, the uniqueness of the situation, the unpleasant responses it evoked.

It's all right, Max, she said. As long as you're happy and hurt no one. But your father . . . he simply hates it.

What's going to happen? he asked.

Who knows? You must try not to let him upset you, try not to get angry. He says things he doesn't mean.

Like what? he asked.

You name it . . . Oh God. Oh Max! Her eyes filled up but did not spill over. He made every effort to gauge the precise calibration of her suffering, so that he could hate or excuse himself for it. It appeared that her deepest intention was to protect both him *and* his father at once.

Max went upstairs and told Nick there was going to be a battle royal and that he would take him to Robin's house for a while.

Max's sister was a clinical psychologist and a pretty cool customer. When Max returned, his father was sitting in the big den alone, not watching television.

Where's Nick? John asked.

I thought we'd better do this alone, Max replied. We don't need Nick for this. Where's Mom?

I don't know, his father said. In her room, I guess. She was here a minute ago.

Max walked around the enormous room, went to the

window to inspect the lawn, the extra acre of woods they had bought in the back for privacy; everything, inside and out, in perfect order. He turned to his father.

Where do we begin, Dad?

I don't know, John replied, not looking up, then looking up. You tell *me*.

After a pause in which he assembled the words carefully, Max said, I recently faced the fact that I am a homosexual.

I'm aware of that, John said.

Well, I guess it's time you faced it too. I like men and I'm in love with Nick.

You've got a fucking nerve coming in here and saying that to me, his father snapped. What the hell do you have to tell *me* about it for?

Well, you asked why I moved to Rome, and anyway I wasn't going to sneak around and lie about it to you. We're going to live in New York and ... we'll be right there. Unless you'd rather not see us.

His father didn't answer. Max made another revolution of the room, winding up back at the window, which was a sliding door and therefore an exit. He realized suddenly that he was at an enormous disadvantage, perhaps an overwhelming one. Everything here was his father's.

Mom doesn't seem to care particularly, he said, turning from the window. Why do you?

Because! His father brayed the word. I just don't like it, that's all. Why should I? Who the hell does?

Let's not drag the world into this, Pop, Max said, trying to be as light as possible.

The world is the point, John said. Is *everybody* wrong?

Yes! Everybody's wrong! Max shouted back. And it's not the first time.

That's your opinion, John said derisively. I don't agree with it.

Well, what do you expect *me* to do about it? Max said. Pretend I'm straight? So you won't feel bad?

Yes, John said calmly.

You'd rather I was straight and unhappy than happy with Nick.

That's right, his father said.

And I should keep it a secret.

That too.

Or?

Or nothing. You can do what you want. I don't care, John said.

Max drifted out of the den and into the dining room, which had a dark mahogany table twenty feet long in its center, ten, high-backed, brocade chairs in slavish attendance, six more against the walls. He wandered into the foyer, which like the den was two stories high. The big chandelier from their triumphant trip to Messina was caught in descent like a crystal parachute. He went back into the den. His father had not moved.

Does Nick make enough money from these films to live on? John asked without preamble.

Usually. He's not established yet. Why do you ask?

I do not approve of this lifestyle, John said, and I have no intention of paying for it.

Well, good, Max said quickly. You can keep your money.

How would you like me to come over there and break you in half? John said.

How'd you like to work this out for yourself? Max replied, thinking of Lydia.

They glared at each other, but neither moved and the moment passed.

Max went into the kitchen and poured a glass of juice from the refrigerator. He turned around and raised the glass to his lips. His mother was sitting at the kitchen table listening, her hand supporting her chin at an angle that caused her to gaze out the front window. She did not look up at him.

It went on like this for hours. At one point Nick called to find out what was happening.

He's cut off the money, Max said, but I knew he'd do that. He thinks you're after the Desir millions.

Nick said, Pick me up. We'll spend the night at Paul's, meaning a friend in Manhattan. Tomorrow we'll find an apartment.

Max said, Oh God . . .

I know it's hard, Nick said. But you have to stand up to them.

No, my mother is fine. She said as long as I'm happy and he said as long as I'm not . . .

Just leave and pick me up. Your sister is terrific. She's filling me in.

Max began to weep and couldn't stop, not for the awful things that were being said, but for the things that had been withheld. He did not try to hide his tears, and in fact broke down completely in front of his father. Of all his efforts this seemed to have the most effect, though not enough to make any difference. John never cried.

Max went up to his room to get his things and Nick's. Exhausted, he sat for a moment on the edge of the bed. His mother came in noiselessly and sat down beside him. She took him in her arms and he sobbed against her.

He wouldn't even bend, Max said.

I know, darling, she said, and held him as he wept.

V

IN JULY, AFTER A SERIES OF TWENTY-EIGHT RADIATION TREAT-
ments, Marie said she would spend the rest of the summer as usual in Cedar Beach, at the oceanfront house
they had bought fifteen years before. In the interven-
ing summers the family had met there in smaller
groups for a few weeks at a time. But they had never
assembled, down to the last grandchild, for more than
a few hours or a day like Memorial or Labor Day.
Now, to be with Marie, everyone went. They were
twenty on weekends, including Dan's wife Phoebe,
and Nick, and a few less during the week when some
of them commuted to work. The effect was of a small,
well-run guest house whose boarders had all been invited for a purpose.

The house had been built in the late thirties by a
family named Eagles and was called the Eagles Nest, so
written in an old dictionary left behind and sold with the
furniture. Among the Desirs the name didn't catch on.

After three decades spent in different houses, they called it the beach house, or simply the shore.

The house faced the sea from a low bluff of dunes beside a red-brick lighthouse with a fourteen-mile, two-second light. Down the coast green lawns met the beach with a thin gray strip of boardwalk in between, like gallooning. All the way down, where on the clearest days the horizon came ashore, the rocks of an inlet led into Barnegat Bay. To the north, the eye stopped at the cupola of a large nineteenth-century hotel, half wood, half stone, whose days seemed beyond numbering, but which were nevertheless numbered. In between—the hotel being in the next community—was a row of beachfront houses, and then a small lake, called Pirate's Pond, which once had been connected to the ocean, but which now was plugged up, to seaward, with a jetty of black rocks that arced into the water. Other jetties occurred at intervals of a half-mile, like commas without phrases, and in fact there was little to say about the beach. In summer it was crowded; in the fall local people ran their dogs in the afternoon, the elderly sat along the boardwalk watching the waves and reading newspapers, men and boys sailed catamarans in the wind and fished from the jetties. Then it was empty through winter and most of spring.

The house itself was large and handsome, covered in weathered shakes, with blue-and-white-striped awnings at the upper windows and a two-story porch that ran around three sides. From the beach it had a crab look—the porch stuck out white claws, the red roof was a carapace, and at night two amber porch lights were eyes. From another angle, with Pirate's Pond and its dry marsh behind it, the house looked colonial and sensible, with unadorned, strong green lawns surrounded by banks of sea rose that thinned into beach grass and white sand. At night, when the moon came up—full, fast and so close over the edge of the sea that it reminded him of the sensation felt at the top of a Ferris wheel—it was the moon and the sea of Max's childhood, enhanced by memory. The house happened to be theirs, but he could have been standing in front of twenty different houses all along the coast, putting his face into the sky as into a basin of water, in any summer of his life.

Inside, the house was as Marie had made it, a sweater and skirt of a house, rather than the stately ball gown of the house in Hillcrest. It was pierced everywhere with windows through which the sea, sky, pond, lighthouse and beach, each framed by the porch supports, made bright pictures on the walls. The rooms seemed to Max to contain the reverberant stillness of a particular moment of a particular afternoon in the forties—a moment of warm gold light, laced with the scent of honeysuckle from the marsh and of salt from the sea; a moment in which the idea of many perfect afternoons was distilled into a deep, flawless, bell-like calm.

One morning shortly after they arrived, Penny washed Marie's hair and all of it came away, as if her scalp had turned to cream. Within moments she was completely bald. Penny said, It will grow back, Mom. The doctor says in a few months. But Marie seemed to know better and only looked at the ocean, holding a tuft of the fallen hair in her hand. Thereafter she wore the new wig or one of a number of bandanna caps the girls bought for her. Her head was beautifully shaped, egglike; and if the wig made her look old, her baldness was almost alien in its agelessness. She would not let her grandchildren see her without the wig or a cap, but a few times, for emphasis, she suddenly pulled off whichever she was wearing as if exposing something shocking or macabre.

As another result of the radiation, her speech returned, partially, along with some of her mobility. But as a statement she would hold up her lifeless right arm with the left, and let her hand drop like a stone into her lap. Her right foot dragged behind her when she walked, but the leg still supported her.

Robin came back from the food shopping one morning with an armful of giant daisies, which for some indeterminate time had been Marie's favorite flower. Robin put them, efficiently, into a large ceramic vase that stood on the living room floor. For the rest of the morning Marie sat on the rug, the daisies strewn around her, rearranging them with one hand, sometimes folding the long stems back or biting them off with her teeth. Max asked if he could help but she waved him away.

Later when Penny brought her downstairs again she was depressed, apparently because the children were all on the beach and the house was empty and quiet.

I ... She started every remark with the sound. I ...

What is it, Mom?

She began to cry. They went through a litany of things that might be bothering her, never mentioning the obvious—fear, anxiety, the cancer, pain, death. Did she want her bath? Was she hungry? Marie gave them an angry look and puffed out her cheeks.

You're worried your cheeks are going to swell from the steroids, Penny said. At times his sister was so quick Max thought she could read her mother's mind. Marie raised her eyebrows and nodded enthusiastically, as she had in charades. Since the first seizure she had enhanced her range of facial expressions and become an actress.

They're hardly swollen at all, Penny said, a mild lie to which Marie rolled her eyes. To divert her now, Penny suggested they spend the rest of the morning at a nearby flea market.

Increasingly, as Marie lost her ability to talk, shopping became a direct and adequate expression of being. She shopped, therefore she was. She tended now to buy on whim, easily and with no regard for cost. To pay a high price for quality was a statement of philosophy, accompanied by a shrug and a wave of dismissal. She was ill, she was dying, but she could afford to buy anything. That morning she bought a twelve-foot catamaran. She had heard John agree to get one for the children next season. She considered the intention thoughtless. Where would she be next season? She called Max aside and pointed toward the ocean five or six times before he understood she meant the line of catamarans moored on the beach and not the water.

I . . . a red one, she said, and indicated her eyes, meaning she would be able to see a boat with red sails from the porch. It was delivered the next day, accompanied by an instructor. John put Penny's son, as the eldest male grandchild, solemnly in charge. Marie however could not see the boat or the red sail from the porch. Max helped her with the binoculars. She caught a glimpse of it and her face brightened. She had followed the idea through, from explaining it to Max, to seeing the boat in the water—hers, as she had wanted it—which was enough. She didn't have to watch it.

One morning Max got up at dawn to check on her. John was asleep, but he found his mother sitting on the floor by an open window, watching the sun come up. He sat down beside her. The morning was clear, delicately colored and already warm, the sea flat and syrupy, with small slapping sounds of wavelets unraveling on the beach. The sun was just rising. The horizon seemed to cling upward to it momentarily, as to a separated yolk. Then the edge of the sea fell back and an orange light bled out in all directions, bathing their faces and painting a strip of color on the wall behind them above John's head. Marie's face was suffused with a sleepy, appreciative look and she rested her head on Max's shoulder. He thought this was meant to mark and replace every sunrise she had ever seen and could not remember. It seemed the combination of the beauty of the seascape and the fact that she must crawl from her bed to face it alone had been, by some dreamlike connection between her and Max, narrowly averted. When the orange light grew pale and turned to lemon, he helped her back into bed, and she sighed and fell asleep.

One afternoon she was able to walk slowly down to the water's edge with Max. Nick ran ahead and took pictures. They sat on an overturned lifeboat and watched the grandchildren in the catamaran, flying above the water. He told her when to wave back. It was, second by second, the last time she would go down to the beach. Later he and Nick smoked a joint on the deck and Max came down onto the porch and found his mother just waking from a nap. Sitting down beside her, he experienced a circling feeling in his head, small gyrations from the marijuana. Immediately, she said, I . . . dinner, then paused and looked at him vacantly. She had lost the thought. They looked blankly at each other, both of them trying to think of what she had intended to say. And because of the grass Max realized what she felt—a reaching back to something that was no longer there, having let go of a tiny trapeze in his mind but missing the catcher's grasp. Now a tiny net of confusion caught him as he fell. She looked at him anxiously. It seemed terribly important, in the seconds that grew longer, that he make the connection. It would be like saving her in a way. Then momentarily, he shook himself free of the grass and remembered she had mentioned dinner.

Jack went fishing, he said. He's bringing back tuna for dinner.

She lay back in the chaise and relaxed, deeply re-lieved. She was able then, as if having got hold of the end of a tangled skein, to unravel the rest of the thought. She looked at him and said forcefully, Sweet and sour, then reached for his arm for help in rising from the chaise.

What do you mean, Mom? he asked impossibly and helped her to stand. She led him into the house and through it into the kitchen. Phoebe was at the sink as they came in and Marie said again, quite clearly, Sweet and sour.

Phoebe said, You want to make sweet and sour for the tuna, Marie. Phoebe brought out a big frying pan and a bag of onions.

I'll get you started, she said. Max put a chair in the middle of the kitchen and Marie sat in it. She watched him peel the onions.

Let me know if you need me, his aunt said, and left the room.

When he had finished peeling and chopping, Marie had him put the onions in the frying pan, in a little oil, on simmer it seemed; sometimes covered, sometimes not. She stood by his side at the stove, making small adjust-ments, jiggling his arm to make him stir the mixture. She had him pour out vinegar into a measuring cup. Two ta-blespoons of sugar. The onions turned pink and pearly. Abruptly she turned off the heat under the pan, pulled him down to her level and kissed him on the cheek. At dinner when the fish was served, Penny said, Mom made this, and everyone ate the fish differently.

On rainy days the children went a little mad with bore-dom. When the weather didn't clear one afternoon they begged Max and Nick to take them to the penny arcade in the amusement park down the line. Max found it much the same, the carousel intact, opulent, spinning on a wave of romantic music, although you could no longer reach for the brass ring coming around by Fascination. Nothing cost a penny. When the rain stopped they were dragged onto the rides—the Whip, one called the Flume that used sea water and drenched them all. Nick and Max were avuncular to a turn, parading their brood through the midway, the smaller ones hanging back or being carried, the older girls folding their arms beneath their new, prized breasts, the boys appearing and disappearing into the crowd like excited scouts on the march, filled with reports of what lay ahead. Max missed the lady in the iron lung and said so: the children would not believe there had ever been such a thing. And the boy with the body of a crocodile, and spider man and other gross-outs of the past, currently touring Europe.

When they got home the three older girls baked a birthday cake for Mary Kay, Jack's wife, decorating it with tiny flowers from the garden. A nice touch, girls, Max said. Later, in a white caftan, he wafted about to their amusement. Uncle Max was so exotic. The birthday party was a big success; the cake, a sugar bomb, devoured. Because "Happy Birthday" was easy for Marie, they sang songs and she managed some of the lyrics. Now and then Mary Kay would slip into the dining room to compose herself. Max did the same onto the porch, through one door, Penny through another, Nick through another, like a French farce. Then John stood Marie up and led her in an abbreviated, stationary Peabody that for the moment seemed real. He led her so firmly and carefully that she appeared to be dancing with him, dancing for the children, all the adults having slipped out of the room.

They went for a ride on the *Mara*, through the inlet to the ocean, up as far as the house and back again. Max carried his mother aboard. John and Jack stayed up on the bridge piloting, Nick and the children sat on the bow. Coffee was prepared in the galley and served on a little table set up amid the fighting chairs. Gulls wheeled and cried overhead, as if having spotted the coffee cake. It was a high, blue, hot day. It seemed they might all sail away; it seemed for a moment as if they had. The sky went out in every direction with nothing in it except a shot-up moon. The glassy sea dropped off sharply at the edge, the coffee scarcely moved in the cups.

Phoebe had turned her chair away and Max saw she was crying, thinking of Dan. A minute later she was fine, even refreshed. Nick pointed out the house to the children when they came abeam of it, a red and white pile above the beach between two jetties. Max thought he saw someone move on the porch, although the house was supposed to be empty; a trick of the light perhaps. Then he thought of himself alone on the porch, watching the *Mara* go by and waving back to all the people aboard.

One corner of the porch, where six chairs were arranged around a low table, was called Potsdam because it had the air of an impending conference. On several mornings, while the sunlight hit it in a diamond pattern through the trellis, Robin sat there with John, listening to him talk, asking questions quietly—a psychologist, although he thought he was talking to his daughter. Several times, through the living room window, Max saw him weeping.

The morning after the boatride Marie was sitting in Potsdam watching everyone when her face began to twitch with a seizure, the first since the radiation treatments. John watched it the way he had watched only a few things in his life—a gale hitting his house, a long, slow accident in progress. After a moment he looked at his wristwatch and timed the attack. At thirty seconds he opened his mouth and tilted his head back to look through his bifocals. He said, It's all right, Marie. Marie reached for a napkin and pressed it to her cheek, as if she had eaten something too cold. Then she relaxed and fell back. John said, Fifty-seven seconds, and enfolded her in his arms. Afterward she could not speak. Max carried her upstairs and she slept the rest of the day.

The following morning, a Sunday, while Robin and John were talking again in Potsdam, when they had in fact got to some important point before which John stood poised and anxious, suddenly they heard Marie calling out. Penny opened the door to the porch and said Marie was calling for Robin, who left her father and rushed upstairs. Marie sat upright in bed wailing, at times emitting small shrieks and screams in a loose pattern of repeats. When she saw Robin the pattern stopped. She opened her mouth in a silent scream, something only she could hear. Robin knelt by the bed and took her hand. Another sound broke loose from Marie's chest, a keening wail that she matched with a rocking motion back and forth. Then, having quieted down, she looked at Robin, held Robin's hand in her lap and raised her eyebrows as a sign she was ready to say what had upset her, was ready to try. Robin leaned close to Marie's face, ready to field any clue, on any level, the best she could. Max, Nick, Penny, Jack and Phoebe had come into the room. But John had not. There being no chance Marie could express herself, she looked instead around the room, pointedly; not looking so much as acting-out looking, which meant, where was John?

Penny went down and found him slumped on the couch in the living room, pressing both hands against his ribs and taking quick shallow breaths of air. It was not clear what he had experienced. He refused an ambulance. Jack drove along the beach road, thinking to avoid the traffic on the highway. Instead cars, bikes and people seemed to drift and glide back and forth around them, everything languid and slow in the heat. At the hospital John was shunted through the cut-and-bruise bureaucracy and into a receiving cubicle. An ECG revealed an irregularity. Hospital rules required anyone suspected of heart trouble to stay overnight. He lay with the back of his hand resting on his forehead, a habitual position. The pain seemed to have gone. He appeared to have the same watchful attitude as everyone else, except that he said to Max, I don't get it. Who's supposed to be left?

On Monday the hospital was able to call his doctor, who confirmed the irregularity, and he was sent home. Marie was aware of what had happened. John told her the doctor said he was fine, it was just anxiety. He was to take some of her Valium.

Do you mind, lady? he said.

Robin said she had been wrong to leave him when Marie called, when he had just got, in that moment, to the point of needing someone, and no one was there. Upstairs, Marie had collected everyone and everything to her. After that, John had no more problems physically, although he continued to sit by an open door to the deck, for hours of every day, looking down the coast.

She counted on Max to help with her appearance. After Robin and Penny bathed her, settling into her chair, she would look at him and daintily touch the side of her head—an abbreviated reference to Mae West's Oh say gesture, which to her meant, did she look okay? Now and again she examined her right hand, which was lifeless and swollen. She held it with her left and turned it over, pinched it, regarded the yellowing nails, then let it drop. Reassuring her with a kiss, he smelled her talc and cologne, which evoked a particular moment of the past:

dressed in a long silk gown, wearing pearls and a diamond pin, a black fur stole over her arm, she steps into the room, twirls around so that the silk circles out, and says, How do I look darling?

He arranged her wig. Max of Cedar Beach. Penny tried but hadn't the knack of making it look real, which despite its cost was difficult. Marie's cheeks swollen from the steroids, she looked very like a picture of Grandma Angela on the dresser.

Robin seemed able to objectify, to help them all by being solid. She never cried. She seemed to focus on the facts of the moment to see her through, rather than the emotion. It wasn't just her background in psychology; it was her way. He thought of a story they heard about her after a summer at camp. Five teenage girls in a rowboat on the lake. A watersnake slithered off the oar blade into the boat, inducing sheer terror, the terror of young girls for the idea of a snake. Coolly, Robin took it by the tail and flung it out of the boat. The four other girls looked at her with astonishment. They regarded this act as evidence of a bravery beyond heroism, perhaps even unto oddity. Whence came this coolness? Her manner with Marie was characterized by a need to understand and a reluctance to pity, perhaps from having studied and treated others. But she was no less gentle. They would look at each other for long moments. He had seen his mother nod afterward as if in agreement to something implied.

In July Phoebe had her fifty-ninth birthday. She was three years younger than Dan who on Labor Day would be one year in a coma. When Max asked how Dan was, Phoebe always replied, The same. She visited him at the nursing home after work, usually twice a week. She said Uncle Frank went every day, sometimes twice a day. He talked to Dan, brought lunch and ate it beside him. Phoebe didn't like it but remained polite. The kids gave her a party—the works. Marie proved again that life was opera by again singing when she could not speak.

By the end of July, when it was as if they had always lived there, Max noticed his father and Nick spending time together. Occasionally, before dinner, he would see them in Potsdam talking easily, gazing comfortably out to sea. Nick's father had died what some would call the perfect death—a heart attack on a golf course—except that he had been only fifty-nine. What had appeared as sudden and unexpected five years before now seemed merciful and clean; a flash of light then release. But it had left Nick with no chance of knowing his father as an adult, and this now predisposed him to John's company. In the years Max and Nick had been lovers, John's attitude toward Nick had slowly evolved from coldly polite to cordial, and even to a level of respect—which seemed mutual—for each other's opposite. It had been natural or at least automatic, when John's children brought their mates to Cedar Beach for the summer, that Max bring Nick, who had in fact turned down a considerable amount of work to be there. Nick was in that stage of his profession which precedes success, being known to his peers but not to the public. It was universally thought within the family, especially among the children, that Uncle Nick, while already glamorous, would one day be a star.

During the dog days Max used the beach and swam in the sea less than usual. The sand was hot, the air muggy, the crowd thick and inane, swathed in oils. He walked through the patchwork of blankets and umbrellas one day noting all the books he saw people reading; books on finance, star biographies and a particular fat saga of the moment predominated, as if these few titles had been passed out in numbers from the boardwalk. Semicircles of middle-aged women sat reading and talking. Here and there a blanket presented a complete family, and invariably, it seemed to Max, the father displayed a birdlike attitude—of vigilance, of unease—an absent air. Max walked through it all directly into the sea.

It was that moment often captured in wallpaper borders and ceramic plates, of a small white sailboat pinned in the reach to a vivid plane of blue and a vivid plane of light blue. The tide was out. He sloshed hundreds of yards across the soft accommodating back of the sandy bottom, the water barely touching his ankles. Flat sheets of it unfurled like bolts of material in all directions, with short crisscrossing dashes of foam that met abruptly and threw up sudden sprays catching the light. He passed through a number of bathers at knee level, the greater number at the waist, a few men and boys up to their necks. The thermocline was a palpable dimension, three or four inches wide, into which he slid his toes like cold socks.

Nick played with the children, a strong machine imported for their use in water. He held them up over the waves, flipped and sabotaged them, each idea exhausted by repetition. Jack's little boy and Robin's two younger girls were about the age Max thought of for himself when he remembered being a child during the summer. How was it different for them? he wondered, turning, as always, and imagining the beach as it had been—nearly empty, very wide and white—as if a filter of years, like a scrim, had been lowered over it. He sat on the beach for a few minutes with Penny—she expected it—and her friends, she who had shared every blanket, every amusement ride, nearly every wave of it with him; who in fact, because of her own strong nostalgia for the same period and place, saw to it that her own little boy and girl now got the same. He listened to the snatches of talk—repetitive, soothing, inexhaustible; he put his face down against the blanket to hear the booming clarity of the waves, until the drone of a rickety, single-engine plane, dragging behind it its message of cloth letters, like a secret revealed, caused him to lift his head and read again, these years later, that Noxzema was the answer.

One very hot afternoon, in the middle of the warmest week of the summer, Max found Marie's bed empty and the door to the deck ajar. His mother, in her nightgown, was lying dazed and stuporous outside on the tarpaper. As he was about to call for help, Nick came out through another door. Marie lay by the railing, her head resting on her arm, her eyelids closed unevenly, like window shades. That part of the deck dropped twenty-five feet into a stone stairwell. They didn't say it but wondered with a look if she had come out to jump. When he roused her, she said, It's so hot, and refused to get up. They shifted her body so that she could lean comfortably against the house, and then sat down on either side of her. A small breeze blew over them like hot cloth dragged across their faces. On the porch below several of the children were swinging in the hammock.

Lying in bed, it had seemed to Marie that the rectangle of light standing against the wall was the way out, if she could reach it. With no particular difficulty she had walked the few steps from the bed to the screen door, which suddenly gave way, spilling her out into the heat and light as if she had barged into a furnace. The heat. It took her some time to identify this sensation, and meanwhile the air and the cotton sound of the beach relieved her of the idea of moving farther. Now, in her view, it was as if she had never left the bed. She leaned, half asleep, against the side of the house. When she opened her eyes she saw the hazy blue sky, heard a drift of sound—perceived and forgotten instant by instant. She thought of nothing, felt nothing aside from a vague sense of disapproval, disappointment perhaps.

Late one night at the end of August, just before they were all to return home, Robin woke Max and brought him into Marie's room. It was a night John usually spent in Hillcrest and Marie was alone. A light from the bathroom shone in on her face. She seemed not to be breathing and did not respond when Robin shook her arm and called her. Her eyes were open but not focused; Max asked if you could sleep with your eyes open and Robin replied, That's a coma. Then Marie suddenly breathed in deeply, shifted and awakened. Immediately she began to cry and to squeeze Max's hand. She cried for a minute or so then relaxed and fell into what seemed like a normal sleep.

It was after two o'clock. He came out onto a dune beside the lighthouse and sat in the sand. He thought of her eyes before she had awakened. He had looked into them and thought, My mother is in there. And for an instant something of what she had been looked up at him. A part of her that he realized he had not seen, or seen clearly, or remembered seeing for a long time, was there in the dark center of her eye, as if he had found her where she was lost or hidden—in a well or in a pit dug into the ground. Her own smallness, tininess, the remnants of her self, had looked up at him.

The night was very warm. The two-second light from the lighthouse took endless pictures in the negative—the ghostly beach, the matte sea, all dimensions lost—then a comparative blackness would return with the muffled sound of the waves. The house was dark except for the dim light in his mother's room. He thought that none of the imprecision of their hope, nor their well-meant explanations, could have any effect on this extreme lack of order. Perhaps she had become immune to the Decadron. Perhaps the tumor had grown suddenly, or shifted momentarily. Maybe it was the heat. But whatever had happened, from what it was to what they saw, she seemed beyond any ability of theirs to comfort her further. He thought then of Dan. She seemed tonight to have caught up with him.

But in the morning, when he came downstairs, Max found her dressed and sitting in her chair, freshly bathed, with a small smile on the one side of her face, and her eyes, remembering nothing, wide open and watching him.

VI

MAX FIRST HEARD THE VOICE WHILE HE WAS SHAVING. A short burst of static was followed by a woman singing a few bars of "Tonight About a Quarter to Nine," and then he heard a voice say, Take a piece of paper and write down what I say.

He paused, the razor close to his cheek, and looked beyond his reflection in the mirror into the corners of the bathroom. A presence had not accompanied the Voice. He was startled to find himself thinking in this new way. He had heard a voice clearly, as if someone were transmitting directly into his mind; and he said sarcastically, Do you mind if I finish shaving first? To which the Voice replied, Perhaps it would be better if I called another time.

The beach house had been closed and he and Nick had returned to their apartment in Manhattan. When the Voice came again, he was driving alone out to Hillcrest to see his mother before Thanksgiving.

I am speaking to you from a certain distance, the Voice said in a chatty tone. You are receiving me mentally. I can hear some of your thoughts and all of your conclusions.

A thought of my own, Max said.

A thought, yes, the Voice replied, but more than a thought.

He asked where the Voice came from. From Iala, the third orbiting planet of the Star Arcturus, the Voice answered, although I am speaking to you now from a reconnaissance vessel considerably closer, just beyond your radio planet.

My radio planet? Max said, and the Voice explained, Your sixth planet, Saturn, is a radio planet, a communications planet. Most systems of a certain size have them. The noise is deafening, but it can be tuned to any frequency, including all those of the human brain.

And why me? Max wanted to know.

I wonder if you wouldn't mind if that was explained another time, the Voice said soothingly.

More bad news, Max thought, but the Voice was gone.

He was aware in the mornings of having had rich, violent and informative dreams. The next time he spoke to the Voice he said, You've been brainwashing me as I sleep. And the Voice replied, This is entertainment and education, but if you didn't care to dream it, you wouldn't.

In one of the dreams the twin towers of the New York World Trade Center began to emit a high-frequency vibration in the key of E, like a gigantic tuning fork. Over a period of days the vibrations got louder. Although the sound was not unpleasant, the two buildings were evacuated. One clear bright night the vibration was greatly increased. Roller skaters circling the smooth marble plaza across the base of the buildings looked up to see the tops of the towers slipping into the docking slots of a huge ship of lights from space, a ship that covered the lower third of Manhattan. In many languages it was announced to the city below that those who wished to leave Earth could take the elevators to the top of the towers and come aboard.

Nick complained that Max was talking in his sleep, sometimes giving a litany of responses—Yes, no, I don't think so, of course not—as if in endless interrogation. One morning he found Max's name written in pencil over the light switch by the front door—Max Desir. As Max was rubbing it off he recognized his own handwriting. When he asked the Voice why he might have done this, the Voice said it didn't know; this was not part of the program.

He demanded information from the Voice about Iala, the third orbiting planet of the Star Arcturus, in order to balance the shared intimacies, the pillaging really, of his mind.

Well, life on another planet, the Voice enthused. So much that is different, so much that is the same in a different way. On Iala they watch Earth as you watch television. Using Saturn, a commercial system tunes in human eyes at random, then assembles and edits programs that are broadcast to the public. Example: the lengthy preparation and service of meals on Earth is enormously popular to Ialans, who have, amongst other things, this cultural, psychological and biological difference from humans: they eat alone in private cubicles and defecate together at table.

You're joking, Max said.

Why no, the Voice continued. To share a meal with someone is the greatest intimacy. Ialans procreate by ingesting a particular part of each other's anatomy, which then is quickly regenerated, sometimes twice in one night. Consequently, your fetish for cooking and eating is equated with foreplay.

The transmissions were always short, lasting perhaps a minute or two; and they began and ended abruptly. Max asked why.

This is caused by a time differential—the Voice was pleasant—which interrupts transmission in an apparently random warp perceived by each side in a different time scale. As, for instance, the hummingbird sips the flower, while the flower cannot see the bird. As a matter of fact, Ialans themselves are birdlike; they can fly.

In his mind Max saw a tall, honey-colored man, with huge green eyes and long curly lashes, a green band around his neck, otherwise naked, with two enormous wings of leaflike ebony feathers folded across his back.

The eyes are not always green, the Voice corrected, or the feathers black, but you get the picture.

He saw then a gorgeous birdlady, her wings a miracle of delicacy, piling quantities of light on a green baize gaming table in front of her.

The Queen of Iala, the Voice declared, wagers that Earth will boil. Further, she bets that Mars will have enough time and heat before Helios dies to bring itself to the point of sensate life, at the least. For each additional era after that the Queen receives one credit. She retains as well certain salvage rights to Earth's debris. . .

The transmission faded out.

✤

The telephone rang. He said hello.

What's the number today, baby, a man's voice said on the other end.

✤ ──────────────────────────────

The number? Max repeated.

Come on, baby, the man insisted. Gimme today's number.

After a moment Max said, 279, because those three digits popped into his head.

Hot number, the man said with real satisfaction in his voice, and hung up.

A moment later the phone rang again. Is Massimo there? a man inquired.

Nobody ever called him Massimo except his brother Jack when cute. Who's calling? he asked.

This is Clive, the voice replied.

I'm sorry, Max said after a moment. Do I know you? Isn't this 2222?

No, it's 2223.

After a silence, Clive said, Sorry to bother you, and hung up. But the next day he called back. He said, This is Clive. I called you yesterday by mistake and I just wanted to apologize for disturbing you.

Max didn't say anything.

Do you mind me calling you back? Clive asked.

No, I don't. But why did you?

I don't know, Clive said. Another pause. I guess I liked your voice . . . You have a nice voice.

Later Clive had two stories for why and how he had called Max. In one, a simple random mistake in dialing had been followed by an inclination to call back: pure chance. In the other, slightly more devious version, Clive had seen Max downtown a number of times, had got his name and looked it up in the book. In differing moods, Clive swore and forswore this story, dangling before Max the possibility of unseen admirers and their schemes. He was inclined to think of the phone call as accidental, and it seemed at first that the fragility of the connection was reason enough to preserve it. For twenty-four hours the whole affair had hung like a spider from the last digit of his telephone number.

Clive called again the following week, and the question became, why did he bother? Did his tenacity signify richness or emptiness in his life? Was he perhaps a gargoyle?

The usual affability accrued. Conversation ranged to other things but was never far from sex. Max told him about Nick. It was not that this didn't matter; rather, it was not supposed to seem to. Clive continually asked to meet him and Max's inclination was to refuse. Why? Clive asked. What are you afraid of? This went on for weeks before Max agreed to a meeting.

He began to rethink his telephone impression the moment he walked through Clive's door. A thick, woody incense filled the air; coming into it was like putting his head under water, into a sudden change of atmosphere— foreign, warm and sexual. Three rooms, all painted white, were lit with candles and amber lamps. A small jazz orchestra played quietly in another room. On a small table in a corner he spied clutter. Clustered around a votive candle were a pile of sweets, dried flower petals, a thimble of liquor, a stack of coins and a picture of a black woman in robes. Max asked who it was and Clive replied that this was Santa Barbara Africanna, the Black Madonna.

On the other side of the room a second table was laid out in a similar way, with sweets, colored beads, liquor and money. But here the attraction was the picture of a Russian icon, a Virgin encrusted with metal and jewels, holding up two heavily ringed fingers in benediction.

And this one? Max said, walking over. Who's she?

That's Freida. She must have everything Santa Barbara has. They're very jealous.

❧ ─────────────────────────────────

He looked at Clive. Isn't that voodoo? he said. Do these girls help you?

It's not voodoo, Clive said, and abruptly offered him something to drink. He went into the kitchen. Max opened a glass door that gave onto a small balcony. The view was of midtown, twelve flights up looking north, with black shapes picked out in bright, boxy constellations. A twelve-foot digital clock in the Fifties gave him time, gave him weather. He stepped outside. By leaning out over the railing he could see a big moon—the hunter's moon—rising at the end of Forty-eighth Street as if over the notches of Stonehenge. Clive came out and handed him a glass.

Max, he said. To you.

Clive appeared to have decided, as a result of who knew what personal disappointments, that the disposition of his own ego toward another, either in place of love or as a start to it, was enough. He seemed only to want to please Max. He presented small but considered gifts nearly every time they met, things he had come by in the store where he worked. And in drugs, whatever was wished. Beyond that, his manner in everything but love-making was submissive. Returning up some conversational lane he would approach like a pup and lay a compliment at Max's feet—about his looks, or his clothes, his way—with a transparency that seemed only to reflect some true need to idealize and praise. And Max would say, What does all that mean? You lay it on so thick, who could believe it?

Clive functioned totally at guileless levels. He seemed unable to dissemble anything, blurting it out instead in a fit of imagined guilt, all subtlety dropped in a rush toward simple affirmations or denials. When Max had been reminded, by certain aspects of their conversa-

tions, of the attitudes and responses of his young neph-
ews and nieces, he asked Clive about his family.

I had five brothers, Clive said. I was the youngest.
My daddy died when I was eleven. I didn't think he was
really gone for a long time.

They lay together on the bed beside a big window
with the view uptown. A line of buildings along the Hudson puffed out tall plumes of white smoke like ships
steaming up the river. He tried to think back to anything
Clive had said that could not have been the remark of an
eleven-year-old from Charleston. He asked about the
voodoo. Were the little altars in the living room serious or
not?

I like doing it, Clive said. I had this cat and never got
so much company out of it as I do from them. And that's
all I'm going to say about it now.

What's it got to do with me? he asked.

Well, not a thing, Clive replied indignantly. You
think I put some sort of a spell on you or something?
Well, I didn't. They don't do anything bad, Max.

What about the liquor and the money? What's that
for?

They're like people, Clive said. They want things.
You'll see. In a while the drink will be gone.

And the money?

The money, Clive said, is there if they want it.

But all this did not obscure them to each other. It seemed
to reveal in each a few carefully delineated qualities that
the other could see and define. Clive was simple, affectionate, generous, superstitious and devoted. Max was
moody, frank, independent, volatile and appreciative.
These two personality grids seemed to fit over each other
easily. It took months for Max to figure out why, and by

then he was addicted to the sex, the habit, the convenience, the safety, and ease of it all.

It seemed to fit also that Clive was in love and Max wasn't. He would have been glad to return some sentiment, or, considering his love for Nick, at least willing; but it never came to him except lightly, in waves of tenderness and affection. These feelings he tried to swell into something more buoyant, something that might lift them both off the ground, if only momentarily. But it never happened. When Clive said, I love you, Max, I want you for my own, Max said, I don't love you, I already have a lover, you know that. And it would anger him that anything more than sex and simple affection should be expected.

This inequity had a profound effect on them sexually. Max felt as if he had found a wonderful machine of lust, which did not or could not judge, which was constant and would adjust to the moment, the mood and the whim. Clive was in a less comfortable position, the unrequited lover; but access to Max made him feel all the more favored and passionate. He was shy. He had reduced his talk to a set of basic barometric indicators that made conversation circular. This narrowness, which could at times be maddening to Max, was more usually aphrodisiac. There seemed little else to do but make love. He would turn to Clive, filled with demands, needs, quirks, favorite moments to be repeated, and Clive would say, Yes, Max. I'm here for you.

Was there some reason why he should say no to all this? Should he cancel the situation simply because his mind did not go naturally to Clive before he fell asleep at night, lying beside Nick, or because he was not inclined to merge their lives further?

His mother was dying. Two or three times a week he

visited her in Hillcrest, arriving in the late afternoon and staying until after dinner when she went to sleep. Her cheeks were swollen, her eyes small and glittery, the glitter of drugs. Each time she had a seizure it lasted longer—a minute, two minutes of repeated explosions in her head.

Max would return to the city and sometimes go directly to Clive's. He would step into the amber-lit rooms and find the votive candles lighted before the saints and smell the airless perfume, and they would fall on each other and rifle each other's body like thieves. In the morning Nick was waiting.

Are you all right? he asked. And Max crawled in beside him to be held, thinking of these three separate parts of his life—his dying mother, Nick and Clive. I am now in the Nick part, he thought, and fell asleep.

After a while Nick complained that Max was seeing too much of this Clive person. A fine line was drawn between what constituted sexual freedom and abuse of the privilege. This line might be drawn between twice a month and once a week. Max made an adjustment, with, every now and then, a certain vagueness in his plans for the evening. Nick understood. He had also had friends over the years. It did not seem reasonable to be jealous of each other. These relationships, modest and diversionary, came and went, and were, to both of them, preferable to sex with total strangers.

Right before Christmas Clive asked if he could take some photographs and Max agreed.

I know what you want them for, he said. They're for your saints, aren't they? One each, and maybe one for you. Clive denied it but not convincingly.

You know, Max said accusingly, I feel them in me

when we fuck. Just at the end when it gets real good.

Who? Clive said.

Your girls. They arrive just before the end and get off with us. I can almost hear everyone moaning.

Clive said, I don't know, Max. You have this way of making it sound so strange . . . It's not like that.

The pictures came out well and Clive had one of them mounted on wood in the carpenter shop at the store. It went up on the wall in the bedroom.

I got this man on my wall, Clive said. I can lie in my bed and look at it, Max . . . There's something, I don't know. I feel like you're here. It's company when I'm alone.

Later he asked if he could have some of Max's hair.

No, you can't have any of my hair. Max was angry and startled. What for? For them?—meaning the saints. What the hell *is* this?

I just want part of you here, Clive said. It's not bad, Max, it's good. They like you. They like you just like I do.

What do you mean, they like me? I got enough trouble without having voodoo saints for girl friends.

Sometime later, without a word, Clive snipped off a lock about two inches long from the back. Max had been drifting in and out of sleep. Now suddenly he came awake. He jumped up on the other side of the bed, came around to Clive and slapped him hard on the side of his head.

You son of a bitch! he shouted, grabbing him by the shoulders and throwing him against the wall. Who the fuck do you think you are, coming at me with a pair of scissors?

Clive pressed back against the wall, the lock of hair in one hand, the scissors in the other. He let the scissors drop to the floor. He held out the hair to Max.

Please, Max, I'm sorry . . . I didn't mean it.

You did! Max screamed. You just took it. I said no and you did it anyway!

Max, please. I'll give it back.

Give it back? You complete asshole. Max slapped him again.

Please, Max, I'm sorry. Don't. It was wrong . . . I'm sorry. He came up to Max and leaned against him. Please, he said, and started to cry.

Get rid of them, Max said.

What do you mean?

The saints. Get rid of them or I'm not coming back.

Tears running down his cheeks, Clive said, Please, Max, don't . . . I can't.

Abruptly, Max started to put on his clothes. Clive sat on the edge of the bed, still holding the lock of hair between two fingers, afraid to put it down lest it scatter and go for nothing.

Oh God, why did I have to do that? he said. Why did I have to *do* that?

Max pulled on his pants, socks and one boot. He sat on the bed, his head down for a moment, before putting on the other one.

Max, don't go . . . You're scaring me. Clive took hold of the boot. Look, you have to forgive me, he said in a fresh tone. I just made this awful mistake.

I know, Max said. I was here.

Well, sometimes I make these bad mistakes. I don't know. People tell me sometimes I say something or do something bad, and I know what they mean. It just happens . . . like before I think about stopping it, I just do it. And then I say, how could you *do* that . . . you must be crazy!

It's the saints I'm talking about, Max said. You play house with these two spirits and I don't want to be dragged into it. He snatched the boot away and threw it down. And supposing, he continued, suppposing I suddenly turned around, or jumped up when you were chopping my hair, you jerk.

Clive held out the lock of hair, offering it back. I'm sorry, he said. I'll never do anything like that again. And you can keep the hair . . . if you like.

They sat there for a moment, neither of them speaking. Clive put the lock of hair on the table by the bed.

You've got to back off, Max said. I can't stand all this devotion.

It seemed the room was calm again. The orchestra played inconspicuously in the corner. He fell back on the bed. Clive lay down and touched him, and Max thought, Here I am in the part about Clive.

VII

THE MOST IMPORTANT GIFT THAT CHRISTMAS, 1978, WAS A trapunto tapestry, about two feet by four feet, made by Robin's sixteen-year-old daughter Andrea, and presented to Marie and John. It was a family tree, depicted in quilted outline, with intricate roots and branches, the roots lettered with the names of the four grandparents, on the trunk John and Marie, and on each of the four branches Jack and Mary Kay, Robin and Pat, Penny and Tom, and Max and Nick. At the top smaller branches and twigs bore the names of the nine grandchildren. Everyone including Marie exclaimed over it and Max and Nick beamed at each other across the room. Later Jack said he knew there would be trouble as soon as he saw Nick's name with Max's. But at the time John didn't seem to care and Marie obviously couldn't see the lettering. She saw it was a quilted tree and thought that was perfect.

When everyone had presented gifts to her, Marie, with Penny's help, presented hers—the result of two months of shopping by wheelchair with Greta. To Max she gave an electric typewriter and a fleece-lined coat. To Jack a watch. To Robin, Penny and Mary Kay she gave her three most valuable pieces of jewelry. To the men, Pat, Tom and Nick, went an array of shirts, ties, sweaters, jackets, luggage, a statue. It was difficult to see what she gave to her grandchildren because they all opened their gifts at once. Some of it, her needlepoint, which had been finished before the seizures, had been made into small hangings and pillows of flowers and birds. A tall doll's house was so realistic, complete and still that Max got dizzy looking into the back of it; also an electric car for young John III, sports equipment, clothes, watches, games, dolls, savings bonds, a pearl necklace. Marie had been given an extra dose of Decadron and seemed composed and focused throughout, wavering only when she presented her gift to John, a gold ring, monogrammed with the initials *JD*; she shrugged as she watched him open it, with an expression of bewilderment and disappointment on her face, as if after so many years of gifts, this last could never be enough. John gave her a gold bracelet with a heart dangling from it that read, *Always My Mara.*

The difference about her now was that she didn't seem to notice them unless she was called, out of a distant, empty daydream. A new inertia caused her to sit quietly and passively in her chair and to sleep a great deal. On good days she was both placid and focused, without the anxiety that awareness usually brought. At such times they would speak to her, a direct communication across the usual miles of separation. In these moments she seemed like an emissary from her self, suddenly present or not when she awoke, as if she was able to step out of what she had become, to peer from the ruined door for a moment; or at least, through a series of threats and bribes to herself, could contrive to get a message to the outside. As with earlier stages this one had two qualities to it, two values that were apparent on a good day or a bad day, when she was either closer, to them or further away. When she did speak or sign to them they acted immediately on whatever it meant. One day, in an effort to appease her anxiety over a misunderstood gesture, they changed her housedress three times and altered the left strap of her brassiere. She had meant only to tell them she wanted to be patted with her perfume, White Shoulders.

Right after Christmas, John took her out to have the tapestry framed; subsequently it came back edged in dramatic black lacquer with a thin stripe of gold—a cross between a decree and a funeral announcement, but smart. Max set up the ladder in the den and took down all the prints, plaques, needlepoint, photographs, silhouettes and inspirational sayings from the main wall—the whole pictorial archive of the family, now summed up in this new piece, the largest and therefore the center of a new arrangement. John suggested the tapestry be raised a few inches and Marie put her hand to her mouth, not in alarm but conversationally, at the risk Max took in standing at the top of the ladder.

Later when he and Nick left, Marie was quiet and John asked if there was something wrong. She said no and waved away the whole idea, which he interpreted to mean, yes, there was something, but she preferred to withhold it.

Is it the tapestry? he asked, pointing up at the tree. She looked at him, then up at the wall. She lifted her chin in the old way, meaning, What about it?

Well, the lettering, John said, as if she had actually spoken.

She squinted in the direction of the tapestry, meaning it was too far away for her to see distinctly.

You know that Nick's name is on there with Max's, John said, going over to it. Do you know that? He took the tapestry off the wall and brought it over to her.

She looked at it, leaned toward it and peered at the branches. Max Desir and Nick Flynn, she pointed silently to the syllables. She nodded and sat back in her chair.

After a moment John said, Do you think his name should be on there?

Perhaps he had waited too long to ask. Marie looked at him again and frowned. What was he talking about?

The name, John said, something like exasperation in his voice. Nick Flynn's name is on the tree. . . . It's a family tree, Marie.

His impatience made her cross. Again she waved him away, and John leaned the tapestry against the wall.

Marie's younger brother Frank and his second wife Helen walked in the back door. They came Saturdays from Long Island, right after their visit to Dan in the nursing home. Marie had not been to see Dan since before Thanksgiving and whenever Frank arrived she looked at him inquisitively until he said, He's the same, Sis, and then she looked away.

They all watched television. Frank was the first one outside the family to see the tapestry. He said it was beautiful, then he saw Nick's name, read it out loud and said, Why is Nick Flynn's name on here with Max?

In the kitchen John pretended not to hear. How about another drink, Frank? he said, and Frank said, No, we better get started.

Later when Robin came in and noticed the tapestry leaning against the wall, John said, Max put it up today. I took it down.

You took it down . . . why? Robin later repeated this all to Max.

John threw up his hand, immediately angry. I don't want everybody asking me who Nick Flynn is, he said. It's my house. It's my wall. I don't want *My son is a homosexual* written on it.

Oh Dad, come on, Robin said. Who's going to see it?

Well, your uncle Frank was just here and asked me why Nick's name was on there with Max's, dammit. I don't want them looking at that tree and asking me who the hell's Nick Flynn. I want his name off that tree or it won't go up on the wall.

Now wait a minute, Robin said. It's not something you can do just like that. They're . . .

They're not married, he interrupted her.

Do you expect them to be married? she asked. They've been together fifteen years.

Well, what do I say when people ask? he said. You tell *me*.

If you have to say something, say Nick is like a son to us. . . .

So why would he be on the branch with Max? he said. Like a son to us or a wife to Max?

Why are you making such a big deal out of this? She went back a little. Hardly anyone comes in here and it doesn't matter what you say.

I have a board meeting of the Cadets here tomorrow. There will be eleven men here. I don't want every Tom, Dick and Harry asking me about my son and this man.

Later that afternoon John asked Andrea, through the reluctant Robin, to erase Nick's name from the branch, to which Andrea replied that her grandfather could do what he liked with the tapestry, she didn't care, but she wasn't going to erase anything. Then Sunday morning John moved a seascape from another room to the empty space on the den wall and told Robin to put the tapestry away. As she was going out the door she said that removing this symbol of his relationship with two people was the same as removing the people themselves. Did he understand that? She said that the seascape he was hanging in place of the tapestry represented the gulf he was putting between himself and Max and Nick, and that in this case it was filled with purple water.

When Max returned with Nick for dinner that evening, the first thing he did was peek into the den at the new arrangement. He saw the seascape. Where's the tree? he asked.

There's a problem about that, John said. I was going to talk to you about it after dinner, with Nick. But all right, he said, turning and walking into the den, why don't you tell Nick to come in? And Max, immediately wary, said, You tell me about it first and I'll tell Nick. He followed his father into the big room.

I took the tree down, John said, and put his hands in his pockets.

Why did you do that? he asked.

I did it because I didn't want Nick's name on the tree with yours.

You took it down, Max repeated—as if for an official record that now silently and suddenly fell into session around them—you took it down because you don't want Nick's name on the tree with mine.

That's right, his father said. It embarrasses me. I don't know why I have to have it written on my wall that my son is a homo sexual.

I'm very surprised, Max said evenly. I thought we had covered this.

Well, we have. But you see—his father was suddenly aggressive—it's when people come in here. He peered across the room as if squinting at the tapestry. Who's Nick Flynn? he said. Is he part of my blood? What am I supposed to say? Why do I have to say it?

Look, Max said. I don't care what you say. But have you thought about our reaction? Did you think about what Nick would think? Don't you care about the way we feel?

Yes, I do, John replied. That's not the point . . .

What is the point? That you won't be embarrassed in front of your friends? Is *bella figura* the point?

What am I supposed to do? John demanded. You can be anything you want, and so can Nick. But not on my wall.

Why do you say it like that?

Why do I have to advertise it?

It sat here for a month, Max said. Why, with everything that's happening in this house—

Let's keep our voices down, his father said. We don't want your mother to hear this.

And what did she say about it? Max asked.

Nothing . . . I don't think she understands.

What the hell do you know? Max said, and they looked at each other across two yards of carpet.

Max, I'm sorry. You're my son and I love you, no matter what.

I'd rather have a little common sense and decency.

What do you mean by that? John said.

If you loved anybody you'd realize what you're doing.

You and Nick—his father began.

Me and Nick are part of this family, Max cut in. Whether you see it that way or not. He just spent the summer taking care of Mom just like everyone else. . . . He was family then and he's family now.

Whoever heard of two men being on a family tree together?

What a hypocrite you are, Max said.

I don't want his name with yours on that tree, John repeated.

But it *is* on the tree. That's the way it is.

Well, I don't have to like it, or advertise it, John said.

No, you don't. It's your house. Do what you want. He turned to leave. His father called him back. A crowd of demons knocked at the door, rang the bell, flicked the window shades, tipped over furniture.

I don't want to talk about it anymore, Max said. I think it stinks. I don't think you know what you're doing.

Yes, I do, John started to say, but Max left the room.

Throughout dinner he thought of things he would like to say to his father but couldn't, not in front of Marie, or Nick, who certainly knew Max was angry about something, but didn't know what it was. John cut Marie's food into tiny pieces. It was clear that Penny, who had arrived just before dinner, knew what had happened. She nervously presided over the meal as if hired for the occasion.

Max told Nick as they were driving back to Manhattan. Nick was surprised, then incredulous and quiet for most of the ride. By the time they reached the bridge he was angry and when they got through the apartment door Nick started to cry. It seemed to mean that no one in the family cared enough to defend him.

What about the others? he said. How could they let him do it? He takes my name down like I don't exist. I can't believe it.

It was surprising even to Max that it mattered so

deeply. He called Jack and then Robin to ask what they knew, which was only that each of them had pleaded with John to put the tapestry back on the wall. Robin said she had been very specific, explaining what it meant and what the results were likely to be. Jack had even predicted to his father that he might lose Max, and certainly Nick.

It's very simple, Max said. Either he puts the tapestry back on the wall and apologizes to Nick, or after Mom is gone I'll never see any of you again.

Us? But why penalize us as well? his brother said. We tried to stop him, Max. We tried everything.

You should have stopped him. You should have held him down. You should have stuffed his mouth with rags.

I don't think he knew how strongly you would react, his brother began. In their conversations Jack tended to speak in long sentences and Max tended to interrupt him.

I thought you said you told him that, Max said. Maybe you mean that *you* didn't know how I would react.

It's a horrible thing, Jack said.

What would you do, Max said, if Dad took Mary Kay's name off the tree? What would you do?

It's not the same thing.

Don't give me that shit. It's exactly the same. If you can't see that you're no better than he is.

How can you say that, Max? Your homosexuality means nothing to me one way or the other.

This happened, Max said, because you and Robin and Penny didn't face him together and say it was wrong.

But we did!

Penny didn't say a word, not to him or to me. Not a fucking word. She's too busy being a daughter to be a sister.

You can't blame Penny for this, Jack said.

Why not? I blame everyone. What the hell is this?

Am I less than you? Are you better than me? Do you think Nick and I can be erased?

No, of course not.

Either you talk to him now, Max said, or I'll never see you or your wife or your kids or any of you again.

But Max . . .

If Nick and I mean anything to you, you'll say it. You all will. You'll threaten him and convince him he's wrong.

But we tried, Jack said.

Oh fuck, Max said, and hung up.

He had a similar though less excitable conversation with Robin.

Can you tell me, he asked, why he had it framed and then helped me hang it?

It was Uncle Frank, she said. He came in and saw it. I think he and the Lady Helen were the only ones to see it. When Frank asked about Nick, Dad suddenly realized everyone would ask. And he's having this meeting there tomorrow with all his Naval Cadet friends. Of course he thought that every time someone asked about it he would have to deliver a homily on homosexuality.

If the rest of the family doesn't back us up, we're leaving, he said.

Oh, I don't blame you, she said. But I'm not so sure there'll be much to leave after Mom dies.

He didn't go out to Hillcrest for a week, and Nick stopped going altogether. It seemed clear from the drooped and anxious look Marie gave him as he came through the door that she understood what had happened. She held on to him for an extra moment, patted his shoulder, held his hand. Lately any opinion or expression of hers however was subject to exaggeration, and perhaps she meant only to register the idea that she hadn't seen him in days.

Other than to say yes or no, she could no longer speak, except on certain days or even at certain moments when, spurred on by some issue or event to make an effort, she was able to string together two garbled words. An extra dosage or hypodermic shot of Decadron, which Doctor Feeney orchestrated to forestall immunity, did not bring back speech so much as a thwarted impulse to speak. Each decline was followed by a booster shot, with decreasing effect, followed by a shorter improvement and further disintegration. The seizures seemed to measure the tumor's growth, or seemed even to be the growth. They struck apparently at random, sometimes two at a time, or two that came twelve hours apart with, then, nothing for a week. The left hand, which had become dexterous enough to sign a will and power of attorney for Jack, attended these devastations in a helpful, yet detached and unaffected way—a single column left standing as the temple fell. When a seizure struck, the left hand reached immediately for a napkin or handkerchief, always nearby, and held it to her face; it pressed the twitching eyelid closed and shielded her somehow from everyone's horrified looks. If the attacks were longer, their effect, both during and afterward, was different. She didn't twitch so violently, facial spasms were decreased and she seemed almost on the verge of control, as had been predicted. Afterward, she was less tired. But during a series that struck over the course of consecutive afternoons, Max was able to see that so much had already been taken by the tumor that further disintegration scarcely showed on the outside.

Instead of coming for dinner, he came now for lunch, when Greta could assure him that John was at the office. Afterward he sat with Marie in the den watching television. She half listened, half dozed on his shoulder. The program was a word game. Two celebrities vied with each other for the pleasure of making two ordinary people famous for fifteen minutes, using words as wands.

In quotes at the bottom of the screen, the word *Needlepoint* appeared. Marie looked up.

I'll pass, the first of the celebrities said.

The other celebrity looked into the vast and vacant stare of her partner and said, Crewel, pronounced crew-el.

Mean, the partner said too quickly and was punished with a rude noise offstage.

Marie pointed to the screen.

Embroidery, the first celebrity said carefully.

Needlepoint, the other contestant replied, and Marie looked up at Max and smiled. A few moments later she was asleep on his shoulder.

Until then, whenever one of them suggested they hire a nurse, John said he didn't want to frighten Marie with a stranger. A nurse was worse than strange and they did what was necessary to organize the situation as it stood. They had all rearranged themselves after returning from the beach house. Greta and the girls saw to the details of feeding, bathing and medication. John and Penny kept a series of charts that John had devised to keep track of everything—the Decadron, Valium, laxative, potassium pills. They planned to have her remain at home and this was made clear somehow. Gradually Marie's room was converted to hospital standards. A special bed replaced a skirted taffeta chaise in the corner. When she developed a bruise that turned into a bedsore a sophisticated air mattress and motor were added that caused the mattress to ripple every minute or so from one side to the other. It was Marie's own inertia that required John finally to hire someone. One morning during her bath, he nearly dropped her. Penny called an agency Doctor Feeney told them about and a tall black woman, named Mrs Washington, arrived the next morning at eight. She called Marie honey and after Marie had opened her eyes as wide as she could and stared for identification, she smiled, lay back, and let Mrs Washington attend. After a few days, however, Mrs Washington doubted she was strong enough for all the lifting and turning that would be required. A woman from Vienna, whom Max recognized from several old movies as *the nurse*, was too old and half the size of Mrs Washington; she lasted two days. A third woman was younger but Marie didn't like her and Penny had words with the agency. Someone strong and competent, she said, and the agency announced they would now send over their best nurse.

The next afternoon Max came in and found a black baby girl in a crib in the den, looking through the glass doors at the trees. Max rolled her over on her back, she looked up at him and smiled, showing two tiny teeth in front, the most beautiful baby he had ever seen. A sachet of camphor hung from a string around her neck and when you put your face close to hers it cleared the head. The combination of the camphor and the baby's beauty was devastating and she seemed already used to evoking a response in everyone. Penny said that when they put her in Marie's lap, Marie had laughed. Her name was Aisha. Her mother, Madelaine, was obviously the source of beauty. From the two faces it seemed possible to reconstruct the features of the father, who must also have been very handsome. This person had apparently run off.

After Marie fell asleep Greta made tea and coffee, which she had not done for the earlier auditions, and she, Penny, Robin and Max listened as Madelaine gave a short and positive account of herself. There was cake. Madelaine dandled Aisha in her lap. She said she had been forced to bring her because the babysitting arrangements had fallen through at the last minute and she had not wanted to miss the work. She said new arrangements would be made tomorrow. But everyone was so enchanted and in a way relieved by the baby's presence and her effect on Marie that Madelaine brought her every day after that. Aisha looked at each of them across the coffee table and smiled sweetly, like an idol.

Madelaine did not look much older than twenty-five or thirty, although she seemed to be somewhere in a corridor of health and handsomeness that stretches into the mid-forties for some people. Suddenly Max went red with recognition. It was Louella. Louella had been twenty years before, but Madelaine was Louella, his mother's cleaning woman from Indian River.

I'll make sure Marie is comfortable, Madelaine said. I'll take good care of her.

Later in Marie's room, while the others were out, he said in a loud whisper, Louella, and she looked up from the formation of a perfect hospital corner.

Why'd you call me that? she asked.

You remind me of someone I used to know. We used to know. Marie was awake now. She looked up at Madelaine, it seemed to Max, speculatively.

Nobody calls themself Louella anymore, darlin', Madelaine said.

Marie was looking at him with her eyebrows raised.

Doesn't she look like Louella, Mom? and Marie looked again at Madelaine, then back at her son wide-eyed.

Do you remember Louella, Mama, back in Indian River?

His mother nodded but frowned and looked again at Madelaine. This was her third nurse in a week; to her they were interchangeable, like the hospital rooms from which they came. She reached out and patted Madelaine's hand. She then tried to say what Max thought was the baby's name.

Aisha, he repeated, and she nodded again, as if that were the issue or the answer to any question he might have asked.

Madelaine looked at Max across the bed. After she had helped Marie to sit up comfortably, she said, Was Louella a nice person?

She did me a favor once, Max said, a long time ago.

Well, good, Madelaine replied. Then you'll think more of me if you think I'm like her. But what kind of favor could a young black girl do for you? Or is that private?

Yes, he said. It's private, if you're not Louella.

Madelaine handed his mother a glass of juice with a straw in it.

You have a nice family, Marie, she said. You should be very proud of the way they're taking care of you.

Marie half smiled and lay back against the pillows. When Penny and Robin were in the room later, she patted Madelaine on the hand again for them to see. This was her way of choosing Madelaine, and of making sure that she stayed.

Nick would not return to Hillcrest and Max went only in the hours John was out. He wanted to make it as clear as possible that if it wasn't for Marie he wouldn't go there at all. A month or so after the confrontation, Jack called and wanted to know what could be done to restore harmony. It was not apparent if he was acting on his own or on John's behalf.

Max said he didn't think harmony was possible.

Well, is that it? his brother asked. Are you just going to let it all go down the drain?

That's where it seems to belong, he replied evenly.

❧ ─────────────────────────────────────

Come on, Max. You don't mean that. He's your father.

Cut the shit, Jack. We're only reacting to something he did . . . Talk to him about it.

Well, is there anything you and Nick would accept by way of apology?

By way of apology I want a letter of apology, not to me, to Nick. And I want the tapestry back up on the wall.

A letter from Dad?

That's right. Let him write it down. Nick won't go out there until he does. Or afterward, goodbye.

Robin said John agreed to write the letter to Nick but it didn't arrive. The tapestry, however, as a compromise, was hung in the upstairs hall, outside Max's room. Surprisingly, Nick was somewhat appeased, but Max said no one but them and Greta ever went up there. He continued to visit his mother alone. In another call Jack tried a different tack.

He said, I hope Nick isn't going to stop seeing Mom because of what Dad did. That's not right. Doesn't he care for her?

Nick was hurt enough to get angry. What an incredible bunch of people you are, he said to Max. A person could get ground up into hamburger meat out there. I don't give a shit *what* your brother says or thinks about my feelings for your mother. It's all in how things look to them.

But thereafter, once a week, Nick went to Hillcrest with Max if it could be guaranteed John wouldn't be home.

Marie was beyond knowing who visited her and who didn't. She slept a deep, odd sleep most of the time and was seldom out of her bed. Eventually John stopped going to the office except for a few hours a week. Jack helped him, filling in where he could.

By the beginning of May Marie didn't often distinguish between them. She hardly ate and began to run a constantly fluctuating temperature. Feeney said it could not be much longer. He said that if he stopped giving her the Decadron she would die within a week. He said there would be no pain. She hovered each day at the edge of coma, drifting in and out of it like a woman at the edge of a lake she thinks is shallow but which is not.

When Madelaine told him it would only be a matter of days, he and Nick moved into the house. Nick hadn't wanted to but said there wasn't any alternative.

VIII

NICK STAYED OUT OF THE WAY BY WORKING ALL DAY IN THE garden. Mary Kay came by one afternoon and she and Max had coffee on the terrace. She talked about going around to find a funeral home and cemetery, which she had offered to do. The cemetery where both the Desiderios and the Defilippos were buried had lost some of its charm when the Long Island Expressway was run through the middle of it. The mortuaries she had seen were either lugubrious and gloomy or sleazy and vulgar. In one, she mistakenly entered an enbalming room, which fortunately was empty, containing large stainless steel troughs, tubes, run-offs, and drains in the middle. Another place seemed entirely deserted, the foyer and viewing rooms empty. Suddenly an enormous black dog appeared, its shoulders down, head near the floor, a deep, vicious growl rumbling through its bared teeth.

My heart stopped, Mary Kay said. I nearly committed suicide by breaking and running for the door.

Instead she inched backward, and the dog moved forward, slowly, slowly, allowing her to leave. She thought Grey's Funeral Home in the next town was the least offensive she'd seen. In a few days they might go and make arrangements, select a coffin. She asked if he would like to see a cemetery she had found, a beautiful old place with huge trees, ornate stones and statues.

As they drove through the stone gates Mary Kay pointed to a small gothic chapel just inside and said, That's where the manager is, a great huge pig of a man. He must weigh four hundred pounds.

Everything was in bud—dogwood, cherry and apple blossoms, white hydrangea, wild daisies. They drove along a serpentine macadam road, just wide enough for the car. Shade patterns from the trees slid across the hood like veils. Many of the gravestones and monuments seemed as old as the trees: obelisks, statues, urns, crosses, slabs, a double heart, an open book, mausoleums with stained-glass windows and tiny gardens; and interspersed, smaller, simpler, modern stones, here and there a rectangle of turned earth, a pile of dead flowers and ribbons like a heap of bright laundry.

The plot itself had several big trees, an oak and two tulip poplars joined at the base. Max had the odd and immediate feeling he was standing on the site of his own grave. He saw himself and Nick buried beside his parents, if he saw them buried anywhere. One would wind up here.

But it's these trees really, Mary Kay said, looking into the branches overhead. The canopy extended like a cavern of receding green billows, pinned back here and there and pierced with shafts of light.

I saw the stone there, she said, with the tree behind it. The manager said for some reason the plot was improperly marked as sold for over seventy years, and just discovered. It's the only one left in this section.

Nick had settled on the idea that Andrea's having made the tapestry was more important than John's bigotry. They barely spoke to one another but everyone was so gloomy it hardly mattered. John was with Marie all the time, keeping his charts, pleading with her to take whichever pill it was, as if this might make a difference. He still did not seem to admit to himself that she was going to die.

Madelaine was strong, efficient, handsome; Aisha incongruous and lovely in her crib in the den. Greta, relieved of the awesome responsibility of caring for Marie, spent all her time in the kitchen preparing lunches and dinners and caring for the baby. Madelaine seldom brought Aisha into Marie's room, there no longer being any point; nor perhaps did she want her baby so close to death and dying. She said the camphor was for colds, but he thought it was for protection. Clive said spirits could hide in babies for a while but that they couldn't stay there.

One early morning Madelaine woke Max and said Marie was asking for him. He ran downstairs and found his father standing by her bed. Max came around to the other side and put his face in her neck. She was wearing one of the bandanna caps, which smelled of her perfume. The room itself smelled of oxygen and sickness. She put her good arm around his neck and held him, pressing her cheek to his. He told her he loved her and she nodded and let him up.

She turned to John and put her hand to his chest. He leaned toward her, not knowing what she wanted.

What is it, Marie? he asked.

She moved her hand from his chest to Max's and looked at him and started to cry. Then again she put her hand on John.

Okay, Marie, John said. It's okay. It'll work out, I promise you.

John had gone red in the face. He sat on the edge of the bed and held her until she slept.

Max dreamed he came into the kitchen and found his mother by the sink, washing her good cups, singing to herself. He came up beside her and she stopped and said, What is it, dear? Nothing, he replied. It's so good to hear you singing again. This fragment stayed with him when he awoke and he thought, she never sang to herself, not that he could remember.

Aunt Phoebe moved in a few days after Max and Nick. Dan was still the same, nearly two years later. No one made the connection between him and Marie anymore. Jack came every night for dinner. Penny was five minutes away, Robin not far. Marie never looked up without seeing Madelaine and one of them.

Madelaine began to sleep over, going home only to change clothes or get something for the baby. John was exhausted from being up all night with Marie. Madelaine made him sleep upstairs. She told Max she would know when the time was coming; soon but not yet.

He thought of Madelaine still as Louella, someone he had thought of all his life. That she had now returned from nowhere, in the nature of an incomprehensible coincidence, did not strike him as unusual. It seemed that as a family they had always ridden to statistical clichés, doing what so many others were doing or had done that it seemed everyone was living the same life, overlapping in banal and endless ways, being so much alike that they seemed all to know each other, like neighbors, in a very small world filled with coincidences. It wasn't strange to think Louella might become a nurse, and in this reincarnation return to the Desirs and be recognizable only to Max. Unless he was wrong. Madelaine was probably too young to be Louella. She had refused, her head cocked, to tell him her age. He wondered if this impression of her was meant to match Madelaine's intimacy with his mother. It seemed cruel for a perfect stranger to share Marie's death with her.

Nick planted flowers, pruned, weeded, did all the work of the overpaid gardeners except cut the lawn. Robin and Max sat on the terrace talking about John. She said he was the only one losing someone central to his life. They all had someone else, their mates, their children.

He's a problem solver, Max, Robin said. He's kept her alive for seventeen months with a brain tumor. What will happen when she dies?

He'll switch over to the problem of surviving, Max suggested.

Maybe not. So ominous, she said. I don't know what he'll do. The idea is to get through in one piece.

One morning in the last week in May Madelaine woke them early, before five, and said she thought Marie was very close. Max called Penny, who called the others, and by five-thirty everyone was in there, sitting and watching, while Marie rasped out breath after breath, one by one. This went on until midmorning, when she seemed to relax suddenly into a normal sleep. The doctor came in a little after that and looked at her briefly, and they went into the kitchen with him. He said she was about to enter the coma. He explained about the tumor catching up to the edema and then passing it. He could bring her back once more with a large shot of the Decadron before she was out of reach. John asked if there would be any pain and Feeney said no.

The next morning everyone came again including all the grandchildren, some of whom had not seen her in a while. Marie had responded to the Decadron, one last time. Her eyes were bright, calm and perfectly focused. Everyone took turns embracing her and looking into her clear eyes. No one had thought this chance would come but it had, as if they had encountered her unexpectedly in a railway station between trains. Everything about what was happening to her was in her eyes. She seemed to look at each of them with the force of normal speech and with the peace and calm of being there, in that moment. Max came into the room and found her as she had been, as he could remember her being after one of her migraines and a sixteen-hour sleep. Her eyes were on a level with his. They played over his face, taking him in, in a way that made him think of a series of images from the past, images and sequences of the two of them together. He was a baby, a little boy; she saw him now as everything he was. The eyes took him in, through the mask of swollen cheeks, and it seemed there were two things she wanted him to understand, and which he understood. The first was that she loved him. The second was that as she was now, with everyone there, she knew she would never see him or any of them again and she wanted to say goodbye. Max said, I love you, Mama, and kissed her temple.

Later in the afternoon Father Bill came up from Indian River and administered last rites. He stood at the foot of the bed and called to her. She opened her eyes, although it had seemed she was in a deep sleep. She nodded her head once, to all of it in general, and fell back again into sleep.

The next morning Madelaine woke them again at four-thirty. Marie was barely breathing, one labored breath at a time, and had a very high fever.

They sat watching. Jack fell asleep on the chaise in the corner. John held Marie's hand. Robin, Max, Nick, Penny, Phoebe, the three older girls and Greta sat about in chairs brought in from the dining room. Madelaine slept for an hour in another room, the baby playing quietly beside her. Marie breathed every twenty or thirty seconds. They were inclined to hold their breath with her, and Penny and Max looked at each other in horror when they were forced to breathe first. Later Madelaine came back in and periodically swabbed the inside of Marie's mouth with glycerine to keep it from drying.

They watched for hours. Toward midmorning, as if a weight had been removed from her chest, Marie again breathed more easily and her temperature dropped several degrees. Jack got up and walked out of the room. Max followed him. Jack said, We're sitting in there trying to create an atmosphere in which she can die.

The same thing happened the next morning. Madelaine woke Max and Nick and the others were called. They sat for hours while Marie took one breath at a time. He waited for the shift to come again. Every time Madelaine turned her from one side to the other it seemed it might happen; as if, depending on which way Madelaine jiggled her, she could keep her alive. The fever went up, reaching 106 degrees and passing it. Madelaine never took her eyes from Marie.

Max would sit for as long as he could, then get up and leave the room for a few minutes and wander through the house. At dawn he stood at the window in the dining room. The lawn dipped down to a patch of woods. A verge of fern separated the trees from the grass, the whole thing dark green and dripping wet, filled with a patchy morning mist. About thirty large black crows, some of them jerking like toys, others standing or sedately strolling, were arrayed across the grass. It appeared they were just waking up. Little by little, there came a change of light and in twos and threes, and then all at once, they flew away.

When Max came back into the room John had his head down over Marie, sobbing. Max thought she had died. John's shoulders heaved and shook and he rested his forehead on Marie's breast. Max looked at Madelaine and she nodded her head. He went and stood where he could see his mother's face. It had darkened. Soundless white flashes of lightning lit up the windows, followed by distant thunder and the patter of rain. Marie did not breathe. John touched his head to hers and said, Go now, Marie.

Max wanted to be sure of the specific moment, because in that certainty would be the signal that her spirit had left. But the fever had been so high and the breathless silences too long, making several such moments. When, in particular, would the spirit have slipped away, in which moment?

John looked up, tears streaming down his face, and said, She's gone, children. He stood up and he and Robin embraced, then he and Penny, followed by Jack, who had come around to the other side of the bed. It was Max's turn. He embraced his father. On the occasion of my mother's death, he thought. Everyone now was embracing and then going to the bed to kiss Marie.

He stood looking down at her. The color was changing in her face nearly as if a light were played over it and removed. Her eyes were closed, her head straight on the pillow, her face slightly upturned. He leaned down to kiss her cheek and whispered goodbye. As he bent over her it was as if he had put his head down to a small window cut into a thick wall, through which in the distance he saw the figure of his mother. By an acoustical quirk she could hear him.

Max, Madelaine said, and he looked up and saw everyone leaving the room. He leaned down again. The window was gone.

They all went into the den. Max stepped outside on the terrace but the rain was still falling and he stood under the eave of the house. It was seven o'clock. He wondered if she might still be in the house, or if he thought she could be anywhere or anything at all. He went back to her room but the door was closed. The doctor arrived and went in, and as the door opened Max saw Madelaine standing next to the bed. She had propped a pillow under Marie's chin. It seemed as if she was sinking down into the bed.

Jack and the doctor sat at the kitchen table while Feeney filled out the death certificate. John did not come in. Robin was with him in the den. Jack wanted to know what to do next and Feeney said to call the funeral home and they would undertake everything. Then he said, Maybe you should close these curtains when they take her out. I don't think you want to see that. It's pretty grim.

When the doctor left, Max went into Marie's room. The smell of sickness was now the smell of death, nearly a sweet smell. His mother's forehead was cool. Jack came in.

I don't know what I feel, he said, to which Max did not reply. Jack said, That's our mother.

The doorbell rang. A short man with a big head and a face like a Leonardo caricature stood in the hall. He had large flap ears, a flat face and a long jaw like a fish. This ghoul had come for his mother. Another normal man stood in the doorway, his gloved hands clasped in front of him like a waiter. They both wore black suits.

Everyone went back into the den, leaving the two men alone in the hall. Only a few minutes later Madelaine opened the double doors from the dining room and said they had gone.

IX

FROM THE OUTSIDE, GREY'S FUNERAL HOME RESEMBLED A
suburban bank in the neocolonial style. Inside a modest
theatrical monumentality had been achieved despite the
low ceilings. Various-size rooms gave off a wide central
hall lit with torchères. In one of the rooms an old lady lay
resting between viewings, within a bower of ferns and
flowers like the cover of a greeting card. Mr Grey, of the
several Grey brothers, bore a strong resemblance to a
neighbor in Indian River who had been very sweet to
them as children; had in fact been Penny's godfather.
This coincidence had the same effect now on Robin and
Max as it had on Mary Kay the week before. They sat in a
small office. Mr Grey asked for the name of the cemetery.
It was thought they would need the largest viewing room.
This being Thursday, Mr Grey suggested Tuesday, the
day after Memorial Day, as the first possible day of inter-
ment. That would mean a wake of four days. They, how-

ever, wanted three days, meaning burial on the holiday. Mr Grey doubted this was permitted.

They went downstairs to look at coffins in a display room like a candy shop, with large boxes of chocolates, certain frilly lids opened, lining the walls. As they were leaving the house John had said he wanted the best, in bronze. But they let Mr Grey go on. The bronze cost seven thousand dollars. Its interior was cream-colored cut velvet with shirred edges and a little puff pillow. Mr Grey explained a mechanism that raised the body for viewing and lowered it for closing. The coffin's eventual inviolateness could not be guaranteed.

Marie had never actually said she wanted a mausoleum but Max heard from Penny that Marie had told John she didn't want to be buried in the ground, in the cold ground; nor did she want to be buried on the shoulder of the LIE. They asked Mr Grey about building a mausoleum. He replied that they were very expensive, requiring a large financial trust, nor did he think one could be built nowadays that would be completely safe from vandals. Later, when Max conveyed this information to John, the image of his wife's looted tomb hit him with the force of a slap in the face, and the idea was dropped. Mr Grey asked them to select a dress, cosmetics and a picture of the deceased to work from; he would send someone to the house later to collect these things.

John wanted the coffin to be open during the wake. Everyone else thought it should be closed. Penny said, Mom avoided everyone when she was sick. She would not want anyone to see her now. But John said they would wait until they had seen the body on Friday evening to decide.

It was still daylight when they arrived at Grey's, John and the four of them. Mr Grey showed them into one of the smaller rooms, where the coffin had been placed temporarily, and left them alone. John stood over Marie and said softly, No, no. That's not right.

Marie's face had been painted, with rouge and even eye-shadow. She had never used eyebrow pencil; now two half-moons gave her face a look of attention or surprise that seemed ludicrous with the eyes closed. The wig was too high off her neck and too low on her forehead, and even this could not account for its look of mistaken artificiality, of glossy deceit. The dress, a black gown from their cruise ship days, had been chosen for its high neck, but now the cloth seemed to cut into her skin. Her body was imprecise in places, as if the dress had been stuffed with paper. For Max it was not a question of whether the coffin should be opened or closed. Having her look this way, even in the ground, as if there had never been any distinction or beauty in her face, was more than he could accept. He looked at his father. I'm going to take this stuff off, he said.

Mr Grey came back in. Jack said softly to Max, That looks terrible. Max suggested that everyone except Robin leave the room. The only thing John said was, Do you think you can get it off?

Max closed the folding doors and he and Robin went and looked at their mother. The absolute stillness within the casket induced in him a dizzy, druggy swirl; he reached out to touch the seemingly translucent hands, the left folded over the withered right. Like the skin on her face, they had been painted, and when he touched them they were hard and cold, like something on the thaw, flesh and ice. He tried to rub off the rouge with his handkerchief but a fixative had been sprayed on as a final step. He discovered that the skin when moved did not move back. He tried to free the neckline of her dress but it was fastened at the back with a hook. He reached behind to loosen it and Robin leaned over to see what he was doing.

The dress digs into her neck, he said. I can't undo it without lifting her head ... And the wig's on backward.

Max, no, Robin said, It can't be.

That's why she looks so strange. He lifted the hair and mesh covering Marie's temple and showed Robin a piece which was supposed to fit behind the ear.

Oh my God, she said. I can't believe it. How could they *do* that?

We can't let her stay this way, he said. You'll have to hold her head while I unhook the dress.

They had often exchanged such instructions while Marie was sick. Robin hesitated a moment, perhaps thinking it through, then reached down and carefully lifted Marie's head up off the pillow with both hands. Max again reached around for the hook and eye.

Max, hurry, she said. I feel like it's going to come off in my hands. Suppose it did.

Don't think like that, he said.

But it's so heavy ... It's her head.

Don't think like that, he repeated. He unfastened the hook and Robin lowered Marie's head back onto the little pillow. She shuddered and hugged herself. He was able now to draw the material away from the neck. Robin took a deep breath and said, We need something to take off this makeup ... I'll ask. She went through the folding doors.

Max reached down and slipped the wig from his mother's head. Short coarse gray hair had grown back in the last months of her illness though she was still bald on top. Without the wig, which was crimped and crushed on one side, all her vulnerability returned. He would not let his own doubts stop him—the magical taboos, the mystical fears. His mother's body had been processed like an animal trophy of great rarity. It was now what was left of her, dressed and made up as if nothing had happened—no cancer, death, no gutting and draining, infusions of formaldehyde, injections of paraffin and silicone, no paint. Without the wig something was restored, if only the beautiful, unchanged shape of her head, and a certain sexless resemblance to both her parents in old age. But these remnants were no longer her and he could not let anyone see her this way.

Robin returned. She came up to the coffin and said, It's her again without that wig.

She handed him the cosmetics case they had sent over.

Mr Grey is nervous, she said. He just told me they hired a specialist to come in and do the makeup.

Fresh from a gypsy wedding, Max said. The wig was *only* on backward. . . . He brushed the crimps out of the wig and put it back on Marie's head; arranged it. With cold cream on the tip of his handkerchief, he wiped off the drawn eyebrows, the eyeshadow and most of the rouge. He smoothed out the rest of the remaining color and added powder from her compact.

That's fine, Max, Robin said.

He did something else to the wig and stood back. The mortal remains of his mother, bewigged, dressed in black cerements, lay in the bronze vehicle with the cream velvet interior which, like a sportscar through a paper billboard, would pierce the veil. He wished it was over.

John came in with Penny and Jack. John looked at Marie and said, That's better, and looked again through his bifocals and said, Thank you, children. It's better now.

But she still can't be seen this way, Max said. She would not want you to do that.

I can't close the coffin yet and have it end, John said. Mr Grey, who seemed never to be far away, appeared again and said they could open the coffin for Mr Desir privately before each session of the wake, to which arrangement John reluctantly agreed. They now left him alone in the room and as they were coming into the hall the funeral director approached Max.

Mr Desir, he said, I'm sorry. It was the way she was made up in the picture.

And Max said, My mother, in the picture, was going to a captain's ball, not her own funeral.

He went outside. Mary Kay and the others were arriving.

What's it going to be? she asked. And he said, Closed.

Each day and evening of the wake John went to Grey's a half-hour early. Afterward Mr Grey would close the lid, using the mechanism he had demonstrated to Max and Robin to lower the body deeper into the casket, and drape the coffin with a six-foot blanket of yellow roses. By the second day the room was filled with flowers, with an overflow into the room of the lady next door. Everyone they had known in Indian River came to pay his respects. Max was able to introduce Mr Grey to Penny's godfather—Rassendyl face to face with the Prisoner of Zenda. Women his mother's age walked vigorously through the street door: the survivors. It seemed as he looked down into their rumpled faces—short elderly women whom Marie had known for forty years—that any resentment they had felt for the Desirs becoming rich and moving away from Indian River was forgotten for the moment. Mrs Boyle and Mrs Kruger, both widowed and frozen in the amber of late middle age, each held one of his hands. Mrs Boyle said, Your mother was a wonderful person. And Mrs Kruger added, Everyone loved her.

He thought the closed coffin spared everyone many of the actualities of the occasion. A picture of Marie had been placed on a small table. In the picture Marie sat on the bow railing of the *Mara*, in a red sweater and a white angora tam, a soft smile on her face; behind her and because of the angle, all was blue sea, no sky. It had been taken five years before, on a cruise with the Naval Cadets to Lake Champlain with Dan and Phoebe, and was perhaps the picture they should have given to Mr Grey.

The Desiderios took up nearly three rows. They came each day of the wake and stayed until evening. They went elsewhere for lunch, but at the end of the day they returned with John to Hillcrest. The women cooked dinner and afterward did the dishes, leaving only when they had done everything they could think of. They were all dressed in black. In winter they would have produced black cloth coats for the occasion. They had always seemed, to Max, to be dressed for a funeral.

A curtained alcove off the viewing room was reserved as a retreat for the immediate family. But John never left his place in front of the coffin in the middle of the front row. A steady flow of visitors approached him. He did not cry and seldom talked. Every hour or so he knelt at the prie-dieu alongside the coffin. Jack or Max dealt with Mr Grey, arranging things as they went along.

By Sunday afternoon the alcove had been breached by several Desiderio cousins who wanted to exchange information less formally. As a direct consequence of their parents' entrenchment in Brooklyn, all eight of them had scattered to the winds. One was a policeman in Boston, another a florist in L.A. One lived in Hawaii, another in Florida, the rest in New Jersey. Six had come back for the funeral. Two Max knew were gay but had married anyway and produced children. Early on he had advised one of them on the matter, which advice had not been taken, and he had chanced to see the other cousin years before in a bar downtown. Ill-met by moonlight, proud Titania.

That made three, possibly four out of a generational crop of twelve people: it was a network they glimpsed of ribs and hollows, as they crawled beneath the dim, vaulted cellars of the cathedral.

A journalist friend of Jack's came in with a copy of *The New York Times*, which contained Marie's obituary.

MARIE DESIR
Special to *The New York Times*

HILLCREST, N.J. May 26—Marie Desir, wife of John M Desir, president and chairman of the board of Mara Products, died at her home here Thursday after a long illness. She was 69 years old.

She was born in Italy and came to the United States in 1913. Besides her husband, she is survived by two sons, John, Jr, and Max; two daughters, Roberta Quinlin and Angela Rourke; two brothers, Daniel Defilippo, and Frank Defilippo, and nine grandchildren.

No mention of the way she had died; all such journalistic discretion meant cancer. That Daniel had survived his sister was a moot point. Reading the obituary in the *Times* gave it the stature of a review, of a production in which they had all taken part. Max saw his father thank Jack's friend and hold both of the man's hands as if in some great dedication, his head tilted to one side in a manner he used only when delivering a compliment.

On Sunday evening, the last of the wake, John stayed the extra half-hour with the open coffin, and Max and Jack had to help him from his knees and into the car. On

Monday morning Father Bill conducted a short private ceremony for the family at Grey's. It had been at this point, before Grandma Desiderio's burial, that John's father threw himself into the coffin, an impulse that Max saw now in a different light. Mr Grey gave John Marie's engagement ring and John turned and presented it to Robin. This had been Jack's idea. It startled Robin and she wept for the first time that any of them had seen, and everyone wept with her, including Mr Grey. Max thought a man who cried at funerals like a woman at weddings shouldn't be an undertaker.

They stood together in a small anteroom while the casket was placed in the hearse and a second flower car was added to the cortege. Jack had taken charge of everything. John held onto his arm and said in a hoarse voice, You'll have to help me, children. They came out the door under a canopy. The gray hearse, two black flower cars, and six limousines—all but the one filled with people and waiting—were stopped in the moment, as in a photograph. The five of them and Phoebe and Frank got into the first car, with Jack sitting in front with the driver. On the way to St Jude's they drove past the house, and the hearse slowed momentarily, as if dipping its flags to the big white columns, the perfect shrubs, impeccable lawn. John said, Take a last look, Marie, which sounded ludicrous but which was exactly what Max would have said.

St Jude of the Valley was filled with familiar faces, an enormous coincidence, the juxtaposition of all the elements of Marie Desir's life, with a preponderance of Cadets and their wives.

They settled into the first pew as a friend of Mary Kay's sang "Ave Maria" in a sweet clear voice. The gorgeous coffin seemed to hover over the transept like a Magritte boulder, an object from another world, another idea entirely. His mother was in there.

It was the first Mass he had attended in many years and much had changed: the banal English text with its domestic associations, the altar turned around so that the priest faced them like the host of a cooking show. They all took Communion. He was unacquainted with the latest rulings of what constituted a state of grace. He had never qualified after the age of fifteen and, he imagined, never would. After the rearrangement of the row, Max sat beside his father. John stared at Father Bill, who was cleaning up the altar in a distracted way. John seemed connected to the priest's movements by a profound curiosity, for a ritual he had seen thousands of times but had never closely examined. His face was swollen with fatigue and weeping, with all the symptoms of a cold. When Father Bill said, And especially your dear departed servant Marie, John shuddered. During the eulogy Father Bill said, I knew Marie. I baptized and confirmed three of her children and baptized a few of her grandchildren. The Lord says, I am the resurrection and the life. Whosoever believes in Me shall not die. John nodded his head as if the terms of a contract were being explained to him.

Jack had resolved as a last gesture to his mother to see that she was buried on Memorial Day, a bureaucratic dilemma. It had taken all weekend and considerable influence to arrange, including calls to three mayors, a judge, two police chiefs, and the head of the gravediggers' local. Every municipality between St Jude's and the cemetery had a parade planned for that morning. Three of them were diverted; police escorts helped to cut through two more. In both cases the cortege was longer than the parade. One spectacle slid by the other. From the people at the curb came long looks of docile respect, or of surprise with festive traces; children on their fathers' shoulders did not perceive the difference and waved; old peo-

ple wondered who had died so expensively; several poli-
cemen and a deft majorette held back an oblivious
marching band. And on the other side came two hundred
cars with their lights on, two rows of daytime moons,
pallid amid the flashes of sunlight off windshields.

To sweep sedately through fancy stone gates in a
limousine had always been a particular image to Max and
as they threaded into the cemetery he wondered if this
was why. At a small distance from the gravesite the cars
stopped and the hearse and flower cars went on alone. A
few moments later they pulled up to a pile of little girls in
party dresses. An awning sheltered the coffin from the
intense beauty overhead. Chairs had not been provided
and everyone stood in a half-circle three or four deep, in
no particular order. Nick touched his arm. A few of the
grandchildren were crying; only since the funeral had
come out-of-doors was it real to them. Father Bill said,
Lord, receive Your servant Marie, and Ashes to ashes, in a
loud reedy voice that sailed over their heads and flew off
in the light wind. He went on to the Twenty-third psalm,
interpolating the valley of the shadow of evil for the
shadow of death; and ended with the Lord's Prayer. He
asked God's blessing and they felt the first soft concussive
silence of the empty air.

It was here that, coincidentally, the local parade
came to its own Memorial conclusion, with a distant,
competent taps. This military aspect, addended to what
had been at every moment a highly detailed funeral, and
coming just as it was ending, had a profound effect on the
mourners. All the power of theater was thrown at them.
They were overwhelmed by the sound, the associations,
the complete and utter certainty that all are doomed.
It gave them a deeply satisfying sense of the funeral's
completion, and of the achievement in the end of a

meticulous, civic, somewhat larger significance. The tumbling three-notes of the distant trumpet, floating through
the trees, fell into a single long threadlike sound that
drifted farther off and disappeared.

Three middle-aged Irish waitresses in flats, a short bar-
tender, and a blond secretary from Mara Products who
looked like a beauty queen had prepared the house for
the reception. The last words spoken by Father Bill over
Marie's coffin, and she would have deplored their omis-
sion, had been, The family has asked me to invite everyone back to Hillcrest for refreshment before the trip
home.

Perhaps seventy-five had come back. White-skirted
tables were poised to waltz about the principal spaces.
The dining room table was edible. The house at first
seized everyone's attention. Wasn't it her? Wasn't it
beautiful?

Madelaine came, toward the end, with another black
woman, and carrying Aisha. She introduced the woman
to Max, at the same time handing Aisha to him, and saying to the woman, This one's okay.

He took them through the buffet and sat with them
while they ate. Penny came along and snatched the baby,
who went along happily. When Madelaine's friend went
back to the buffet and they were alone for a moment, he
said, I'm very grateful to you, and Madelaine reached
over and patted his hand and said, I know you are. We all
did it for Marie. She was very proud of you all.

If I give you something, Madelaine said, will you
promise not to open it until I leave? She took a small box
wrapped with brown paper and string out of her bag and
handed it to him.

It *is* you, he said. Why didn't you tell me?

I am tellin' you, she said.

Her friend came back from the buffet with two cups of coffee. We can't stay, Madelaine said. She's helping me move.

Where are you going?

Oh not far. I gave your daddy my address.

Can I come and see you and Aisha?

I don't think you'll want to, she said. But if you do, call and make sure I'm there.

He had remembered it as porcelain but it was bronze. The reins were gone. A small piece of paper was taped to the neck: *Max, 1955.*

X

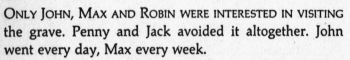

ONLY JOHN, MAX AND ROBIN WERE INTERESTED IN VISITING the grave. Penny and Jack avoided it altogether. John went every day, Max every week.

When the caretakers did nothing to clean up the plot Robin undertook the job herself. A web of weedy surface roots covered the ground like a net. She pulled up long lengths of it, ripping it loose like tattered carpet. Understanding the particulars—the hard stony ground unturned in decades, the insipid grass, roots and assorted tendrils—she returned with her gardening tools. When she had cleared the surface she began turning over the ground with a spade. Toward the center of the plot the shovel struck something hard, just beneath the grass. It was too large and flat to be a stone or rock. Agitated and in a way frightened, she pulled away some of the overlying sod, exposing a flat dirty gray face of cement. In the oddness of the situation, in an old cemetery, it appeared to be an unmarked and forgotten grave. It seemed unnecessarily close to the surface, as if, through the years, it had mysteriously risen up through the ground. And if it was not a grave, what was it? and why hadn't the gravediggers discovered it, or said anything if they had?

She called John, who arrived as if at the scene of a traffic accident prepared to identify loved ones. He had had nothing to do with the selection of the cemetery or plot and might have expected something to go wrong with it. He poked around in the dirt. The stone or piece of cement was rectangular in shape, absolutely flat across the top, about two feet wide by five feet long; too small to contain a body unless it was that of a child. It lay across the plot perpendicular to Marie's grave, toward the foot of the mound of dirt.

What the hell is it? John said with a note of panic, of desperation in his voice.

Robin said, Mary Kay mentioned this plot was marked as sold for years on the manager's map and they only discovered it when she got here.

You mean somebody was already buried here? he asked. We've buried her next to a stranger? Robin! His eyes went red, filled up and ran over. She'll kill me, he said.

Dad, now quit it. You're jumping to conclusions. You don't know what that is. She touched his arm and looked up and under at his downturned face. Let's go find the manager and ask him, she said, and they started off through the maze of plots and monuments.

This predictably calming walk led them to a kind of gothic religious folly that had been erected inside the entrance gates by the builders in 1875. About the size of an eight-room house, it was made of stone and mortar, with the buttresses, spire, stained glass and pretensions of a cathedral. Even standing directly in front of it, the structure seemed still to be a block away. It was used now only as a warehouse and shed; what had been the miniature sacristy had become the manager's office.

Whatever, God help him, was in the plot with Marie, it must go, John thought, and knocked loudly on the sacristy door. It opened and an immensely fat man, all the larger for emerging from the toylike structure, came outside.

Are you the manager? John asked, and the fat man nodded. Well, I'm John Desir. I just buried my wife here a while ago.

The manager nodded again. Next to Willingham, he said.

Well, we just found something buried in the ground there, next to my wife. Right there! A great big thing . . . I don't know how this happened but whatever it is I want it out of there right away.

The manager stood for a moment, perhaps waiting for more. Then he went back into the sacristy and came out again with a shovel. As they were starting off through the graves, Max drove through the gates. Robin came around and got into the car.

You are not going to believe this, she said as a preamble. Through the windshield Max saw his father's distraught expression, the fat manager's toy shovel.

Now what? he said.

Something in the plot besides Mom, she replied. I was digging up those roots and hit something. It scared the shit out of me.

What do you mean, hit something? What is it?

I don't know, she said. Something big. Maybe it's another grave. I couldn't even find the edge of it.

The macadam road made an arc around the section through which John and the manager were walking.

Is it near the grave? he asked.

It's practically on top of it. I can't see how they missed it. Dad is vibrating.

They reached the grave first. The mound of dirt was in the second of its many stages and had a slightly melted look. Half of the rest of the plot had been cleared, and part of that had been turned over with a spade. You could see the beginning of an outline.

The manager, lumbering a distance behind John, approached, stuck his shovel in the ground once and announced, It's an old foundation.

For what? Max said, and John and Robin said, For what?

An old memorial that was never built, the manager replied. He started to dig out one edge of a long cement rectangle. The three of them watched.

This is mortar, the manager said. Been here a long time. I'll have to look it up.

Didn't you look it up when you sold it to us? John asked.

Not marked, the man replied. We would never have sold it to you if it was.

Watching him work, Max felt it was no different from seeing him dig her up. The manager said they would need a winch. John went off with him to speed things up and Robin and Max stood there.

Charming, she said.

He said, It's just like the tumor, and she said, Yes, but this one's operable.

He thought of it also as the remains of the walled city, he supposed, although that interpretation was far too benign for the situation. The manager, his tentlike trousers slipping down to expose a quivering belly of folds, alternated between digging out the sides of the foundation, which disappeared several feet into the ground, and standing on it and attempting to break it up with a sledgehammer. As it was, he explained, it would be much too heavy for the winch.

Would you please tell me, Robin inquired, how the diggers didn't see it? How they missed it? It's practically touching the grave.

Just missed it, the man said, puffing from the exertion and taking the question as an excuse to stop. He had succeeded only in slightly rounding two of the corners. He dug some more, then stopped again.

This was for a big stone, he said. One of them obelisks maybe. Family changed their mind and got a bigger plot. The old manager never wrote it down, just left it marked sold. Then he died, someone else came in and that was that—a secret. He took the sledgehammer and slammed at another corner.

When Max returned the next day an orange tarpaulin covered most of the plot, anchored by rocks and puddles of water from a heavy rainfall during the night. Next to the grave the tarp bulged over a trapezoid of wood planks covering a hole dug around the old foundation block. He threw back the tarp and removed one of the planks. The block had been dug out to a depth of three feet. Near the bottom of one side a corner of Marie's coffin vault had been exposed like a bone. The vault and the block had been less than a foot apart. The block of mortar, greatly reduced in size, sat tilted in the hole. Off to the side under the tree lay a pile of chunks and fragments that had been chipped from it.

The next day it rained again. The morning after that John was there at seven to supervise. By the time Max arrived the manager and one of the gravediggers had got chains under the block and were ready to winch it out. In the end they smashed it up completely and carted off the pieces in a wheelbarrow. As the manager was about to shovel dirt into the empty hole, Max saw him from Marie's point of view—a fat colossus at the edge of the void. Max went over and stood beside the man while he shoveled, until the corner of the vault had been covered again. It wasn't that he thought she could see them, as from the perspective of a window in the ground; it was more a question of being the last person to see anything of her.

He realized that his relationship to his mother had not changed. He had only to speak to her aloud at the grave. After her long illness it seemed natural to imagine or assume her reactions; he was used to the idea of not being sure she had understood or even heard him.

And then at times, infrequently, he imagined she said something to him. He thought she said, Mrs Koenig is being very nice to me.

Who's Mrs Koenig? he asked.

Down the line, she replied.

The Koenig stone, nearby, was a large elliptical slab of considerable style, surrounded by a well-kept, waspishly mature privet hedge. William T and his wife Elizabeth. Died 1913 and 1927. The tombstone, dating from the first death, had thus been the widow's work. He thought of Mrs Koenig and his mother sitting at a small table amid the graves, having tea, getting acquainted.

In this way the Koenig stone stood out from the rest, and he saw that with modifications and refinements, it might do for them.

The proprietor of the National Monument Company explained that they could have anything they wanted, anything at all. Max saw nothing in the display yard that resembled the sort of thing he and Mrs Koenig had had in mind.

People don't go for anything big or fancy anymore, the man explained. His name was Don. Too expensive. They walk in, choose a footstone or a plain slab and that's it, wrap it up. On the other hand, I like to be able to accommodate a project like your own.

Anything you want, he said again. Just suggest it and we'll draw it for you, lifesize, just as it will be, so you can see it.

Robin, John and Max all nodded. Max took out his drawing of an obelisk surrounded by a free interpretation of the Koenig stone, all of it mounted on three steps. Now that he looked at it again, he saw how big it was. It was the sort of thing they might have put up in Indian River as a war memorial.

Robin whispered, Large darling, into his ear. And Don said, How tall did you see the obelisk?

. . . Eight feet? Nine feet? he said.

Don pulled out a pocket calculator and dialed Cincinnati. That would be twenty thousand just for the obelisk, he said.

John said, Holy smoke.

Don took a pencil and decapitated the obelisk at the shoulders. He removed the steps. What we need is a basic shape to work from, he said. Like this.

What remained was the Koenig stone without the shallow apse in the middle or the urn, and done in right angles instead of curves. With the obelisk removed, the space between the two arms looked empty.

I saw a stone in the cemetery, Max began. It's got an urn in the center.

An urn? John said. Don reached up and took down a book of urns. An urn, John said again.

Don suggested they go look at the stone, since it was nearby, which they did. John agreed as soon as he saw it, adding only that he thought the urn should open so they could put flowers in it, and Max said, I don't think we should simply copy some body's stone. Don said, Don't worry, I think I know what you mean. Give me a week to do a preliminary sketch.

They were now to repair somewhere local for coffee. Max said he had to get back to Manhattan. He imagined his father and Robin went somewhere anyway.

The next week they met again at National Monument. They cut down the height of the shoulders, using a curve Max remembered from a bridge in Florence; they fluted the columns, selected an urn that opened from the book, but made it taller, a little fatter. Don said the next step was a lifesize drawing. He would call them when it was ready.

This time Max said yes to coffee but then Robin said sne couldn't stay, so Max and John went alone to a local Pancake House of international standing.

John still looked afflicted with a bad head cold. Robin said he cried at the mention of Marie, or of anything to do with her; although he had not cried at either of these two meetings. It was still unique, as they sat down opposite each other in the booth, for him to see his father in a weakened condition. Robin said the only thing that made him stop crying was talk of the monument or being in church. He had begun to attend Mass every morning at St Jude's. He had already made a preliminary but substantial donation to the parish, and had reserved Masses for two years for Marie on the occasion of every birthday in the family down to little John III, the youngest. It embarrassed him to cry in front of people, in front of his children. He seldom went to the office and did not make himself available for dinner. He said he didn't feel right in their houses because of his moroseness. Except for Max they each asked him anyway, every week. Jack expected his father to find relief and comfort in his grandchildren and was offended when he didn't. Jack said, He's healthy, he's rich, he's comparatively young, and he has a big family. What more does he want?

It had always been said of John Desir that if he joined a club or organization he was soon made its leader. In Indian River he had been president of the Holy Name Society, chairman of the Booster Club, perennially in charge of any and all fund-raising events. Father Bill had built and paid for one of the largest stone churches in the county with public donations and the advice and organizational help of John Desir.

In order to offer its parishioners certain religious opportunities, the church in Indian River had made a connection with a monastery upstate for weekend retreats. John and Marie had gone every year, separately; as had Jack and Robin in high school. When at fifteen it was Max's turn, he felt he had been discovered beneath a rock—a loathsome, sinful vampire in dusty dinner clothes caught out after dawn. Nothing would excuse him his sins—all that masturbation, Louella, the odd wrestling with Scott, plus a whole set of disgusting personal opinions and aesthetics. At fifteen, the nape of a man's neck sometimes made his heart dive in his chest. His uncle Dan's smell, Mennen and man, made him feel he would like to be spanked, though gently and for no good reason. Was God, Christ or anyone else going to bother with such a person?

His own retreat had been a theatrical experience, a three-day struggle to convince himself he was good enough for God. They ate well and kept relative silence, even at night. Every few hours they listened to a sermon especially tailored to the group's principal concerns, sex and guilt. At the end of the weekend, just before Vespers, Max went for a walk through the monastery's apple orchard, fifty trees distributed unevenly over a field of hilly mounds and troughs. Copper light came in at a slant through the wings to one side. The priest had begged them to accept Christ. Only ask forgiveness and all would be forgiven. Only ask.

But really, he thought, did Christ know about men's necks? Did God understand about Mennen? Besides that, it must all be put into words, for the priest in confession.

The clear, fresh autumn air, the smell of apples and grass, the dark web of trees receding on their mounds in the distance, the slanting yellow light, the coarse bark, the gnarled roots, his own skin, the wind against it—all of this comprised a stunning coup de theatre against which he felt utterly helpless. It was quite clear in the surrounding perfection that God was here in the orchard, if only for the moment. Max looked around. He interpreted all this as a sign that even his sins would be forgiven, by the Designer of such a set, by the Director of such a scene. He took it as proof that God did exist and would accept Max into His mercy; would perhaps even go further and bless him, even sanctify him to His own use. Max would become a priest and thereby account for the beauty and purity of the air, the weblike perfection of the trees, the full, fresh happy release into the moment of all his fear and guilt; a holy priest who didn't think or feel or suffer but for Christ.

This air of sanctity had lasted for weeks afterward. But the daily raunchiness and general banality of high school life wore him down little by little. One day a person he hardly knew gave him the finger in the hall, out of pure malice and ill will it seemed, and to Max it was like finding excrement smeared on the temple doors. He was glad he had told no one of his imagined vocation because it enabled him to forget all about it quietly.

John had lately spent several weekends at this same monastery, which was called St Mark's, although he had

had no connection with it or the church since leaving Indian River. Having also helped to build the new retreat house at St Mark's he said he now felt comfortable accepting the abbot's hospitality. There was nowhere else he felt truly peaceful.

But in addition to this new religious habit, John had also rediscovered another old but neglected hobby—gambling. On the weekends he didn't go to St Mark's, or during the week afterward, he drove to Atlantic City and shot craps for hours at a time. He lost, sometimes he won. After years of his being vague about the races, no one pressed him for totals. Jack said he could afford to lose thousands, if that's what he wanted. It was none of their business. At any event the money was not the point. The point was the shift between the monastery and the casino. Miss Sacred and Miss Profane. It seemed offensively obvious to Max, but Robin said the force and directness of the metaphor, the clear-cut dichotomy of good and evil, was classic and very pleasing. It was going to be craps and doxies pushing drinks—to give it its most negative cast—fueled by the adrenaline of chance, or surrender to the idea of Christ. It was in itself a kind of gamble on which they might have wagered, but did not.

They did not know about women, if he was interested, or pursued the many opportunities offered in the casino. Max thought it might be difficult to court a seasoned cocktail waitress if you were prone to constant tears. She might think you odd—although in the casinos, rich covered odd nicely. On the other hand, perhaps it made him forget. Perhaps in the casino, as in the monastery, he was peaceful.

In the Pancake House John asked if Max was hungry.

Have something, he said, and Max ordered an English muffin and tea. His mother in this situation would have quickly, effortlessly struck the right conversational note. How are you, darling. Direct and well-intentioned. He saw his father then as now was not going to say anything so he said, How are you feeling? meaning physically.

John looked out the window and said, Oh ... and two tears rolled down his cheeks. The waitress brought Max's tea and John looked up and said he would have a cup too. She saw the tears and in spite of herself automatically crooned, Of course, dear. She was the kind of waitress who, with a better or perhaps earlier start in life, would have been a nurse. Now and then the Pancake House presented these mild crossover opportunities. People got ill, they cut themselves or fainted, but they never died.

Robin says you're going to church every morning. John nodded.

Does that help? he asked.

Yes, it does, John said, as if he were talking about a prescribed drug. It's the only place I feel right. And at the cemetery.

What about the house? he asked.

I ... I just miss her there. John put his head down, nearly into his crossed arms. He looked up again through tears. Robin had said he told her Marie was in the house and that he talked to her all the time.

I have the feeling, Max said, that she's with me sometimes.

Oh, so do I, John said eagerly. So do I. But then afterward you realize, she's gone.

And the monastery? He did not want to sound accusatory but his father's sudden shift to God seemed in a way cowardly. God would now solve his problems.

It's very nice, John replied vaguely. The abbot said I could come any time I like.

I remember it, Max said. From high school.

Oh, it's completely different now, John corrected. They've got the new retreat house we built.

What do you mean, we?

I built that retreat house, John said flatly. And they know it.

Well, then they should be glad to see you, Max said.

Sure. Of course they are. The abbot is a hell of a guy.

And the casinos and Atlantic City and all of that? Max said. How can you go back and forth like that?

Why not? John asked calmly. It's not sinful.

It's not particularly holy either. It's gambling.

I've always liked to gamble, John said. It relaxes me. It's a change. It's a place to go.

It certainly is a change from St Mark's, Max agreed. Don't you get culture shock going back and forth like that?

His father shrugged and didn't answer. The image popped into Max's head of the abbot in robes, dancing ineptly with a Playboy bunny.

The waitress brought John's tea and Max's muffin and smiled to show how proud she was that John had managed to stop bawling. They settled down.

Max said, I'm worried about that urn. As he said it, he realized the monument was the last, the only connection between them.

What about it? John was relieved at the emergence of this safe topic.

Someone could steal it. Or take the top, Max said.

But John had committed himself completely to the idea of an urn, to put flowers in. An urn appealed to his sense of class. The Fricks had urns. He did not want to stick flowers in a hole in the ground. We'll nail it down, he said. We'll get two tops. I'll keep one in the car.

What about maintenance? Max said. This was now a

normal conversation between them, in which Max asked pertinent, even penetrating questions, and his father gave answers and opinions that then were open to amendment.

They offer Perpetual Care, John replied.

How much does it cost? Max was pleased you could arrange to have the grass cut through eternity.

Three thousand.

Only one payment? By this he meant, what happened in two thousand years when everything was exchanged for light instead of scrip? Would the price for Perpetual Care still be the same?

Only one charge, John said. You pay it any way you want.

After a moment Max said, How much will the monument cost?

I don't know, John replied. I'm not so sure about this guy Don.

What's the matter with him?

I don't know where he gets his prices. Pulls them out of a hat, I think. People seldom cheated John because he assumed they all tried.

Twenty, twenty-five, he added, referring to the cost of the monument.

How much is all that, including the funeral and everything? Max said.

Everything? His father shifted his weight and sat up straighter. Sixty, seventy thousand. Plus the landscaping. It'll be the nicest plot in the cemetery, John said. By far.

The waitress stopped to ask if they would like something else. She wrote out a check like an autograph and dropped it on the table. As Max watched his father absently set the check aside, he wondered what the highest bill was that John would be able to pay—walk up and say, I'll take that, how much? and write a check, or fish it out of a bank on impeccable personal and corporate credit.

Thousands of course, tens of thousands, possibly if not probably hundreds of thousands; maybe even a million. One of the principles of their relationship seemed to be a mutual inflation of John's material wealth. John liked to think he was richer than he was and continually gave that impression to Max, most often through inflated statistics. And the more money he thought his father had, the easier it seemed to understand him. It had been during moments of true largesse, of expansive financial and material gestures—like the purchase of a dozen suits at Barney's, or of a huge car or a jewel for Marie—that Max thought he saw his father most clearly.

It had been John's intention, Max knew, to be lavish about Marie's burial, as lavish as she would have permitted, balanced against as lavish as he dared. He had been so influenced by her that now, with both his life and hers in pieces around him, he picked up anything that resembled her, and kept it as his own. He constantly wondered what Marie would have done or wanted or insisted on, and then did the same. In this he tended to be accurate, if inclined to embellish in favor of the most expensive, believing Marie always preferred the best when she had merely required that something be well made. Max served the purpose of toning it all down, and yet managed always to help John spend even more. The truth was they both believed they should spend money on her now. If she had not taken it with her it was perhaps up to them to send it on after her—an Egyptian way of death. This attitude was also complicated by more personal aspects. Besides burying Marie, John was arranging for the eventual disposition of his own body. He thought of this nearly every time he looked at the plot. He had put Marie's grave to the right of center—with a line drawn from between the pillows—in order to leave half for himself. And unless otherwise specified, whoever else died from now on would be buried there too. Max did not see himself specifying otherwise.

To have pinpointed the probable location of his bones, left in the world after him in a certain spot—beside Mr and Mrs Magreb, and Colonel Willingham who had bought it in Spain—this knowledge had a different effect on Max than on his father. To begin with he tried not to think of it. When it did occur, he imagined himself standing over his own grave, years hence; standing on the plot but also buried in it. He tried to store up the image of being above the ground and in it at the same time—simply dead *and* alive. But the result was the momentary feeling of having slipped by some macabre reversal into the ground instead. For a moment he felt himself fading out, going transparent and flowing like a heavy mist through the grass, into the vault below. It all came to him in the sudden chill he felt just before drawing back.

His father said, How are you making out?

All right, he replied. I miss her. This indulgence nearly caused him to cry too, but he stopped himself. They drank. Max ate his muffin.

John said, I hear you've got a job with a caterer.

That's right.

Well, what's it like?

I serve dinners with Irish waitresses at Jewish country clubs. I pass hors d'oeuvres. I work in the kitchen. I am a waiter, he said.

Does that give you enough for you to live on?

It's all right, he said.

You're the one who doesn't want any help, John said.

Let's not go into that here. Max suddenly sensed the elusive but satisfying appeal of a public scene, the tremors from neighboring booths, that dark, you've-ruined-our-pancakes look. In that moment he hated the disparity in their lives and attitudes, the gulfs between them.

Well, how long can this sort of thing go on? John said.

What do you mean? Max said, knowing what he meant. How long can what go on?

Is that the kind of job you want for yourself?

What the hell business is it of yours?

Don't you have debts?

Everyone has debts.

How are you going to pay them? How are you going to live?

We'll manage. Nick makes money.

You'll manage, his father repeated. Is that the way you want to live?

I didn't plan it this way, did you?

His father was startled. No, of course not. But whichever way it happened, can't we do something about it?

Like what?

Why don't you let me help you?

Why should you?

Oh come on, Max. You're my son. No matter what, you're my son.

That's bullshit. Worst fears confirmed, faces in the neighboring booths turned as if toward a nasty smell. This *was* a scene.

John made a sudden movement, sliding across the leatherette to stand up. Look, I've got to get out of here, he said.

That suits me, Max said, and was up before his father and out the door. He got into his car and with a squeal of tires, drove off.

XI

TWO MONTHS AFTER MARIE'S FUNERAL one of JOHN'S NEPH-
ews got married. In conversation with Penny and Max at
the reception Aunt Clara said, So what's this about your
father going into a monastery? He's going to become a
monk?

Max was astonished but managed not to alter his expression. Penny was less surprised. She said, Yes, he was
thinking about it.

He told us he's going to do it, Clara said, widening
her eyes. A trial. A few months to see if he likes it.

In between his now regular trips to the monastery
and Atlantic City John occasionally visited his family in
Brooklyn. Recently he had invited all the Desiderios to
Hillcrest for the weekend; it was not surprising that Clara
had the latest news.

I think he's serious, she said. Clara was used to the
insidious, inexorable losses and disappointments of life.
But it was deeply shocking to her that her brother the ty-

coon, who had everything—which none of them had—was now going to give it all away. She turned to Max.

He has to take a vow of poverty, you know. Same as a priest. Worse; not even a dime in his pocket.

Robin said John had meant only that they should return to Hillcrest to finish the conversation rather than continue it in the Pancake House, but that Max had run away. This was not the way it was, but Max felt much of their relationship had been determined by misinterpretation. He and John pretended it had not happened, a simple expedient. Max asked him about the monastery. He said he was going in for six months starting in January.

A polite suicide. According to Robin, now standing hip deep in familiar waters, this was Acting Out. John had come up with a plan of action. It was surrender to an idea; the removal of all responsibility. Someone else might have quit his job and gone on welfare. This was the reverse; he was required to quit for God. The church would be his welfare. He would put himself in God's hands.

John asked Jack to take over Mara Products while he was in the monastery. Jack said he would take over, but not just for six months. This was not, supposedly, a strategy of Jack's ambition, but an effort to make John realize what he was giving up.

The same week as the wedding a letter came for Nick on Chinese notepaper Marie had kept in the dining room buffet.

Dear Nick,
Writing this kind of letter is not my specialty; but since I was asked to do it and I have agreed—here goes.
At the outset let me say that I am sorry for hurting you. There never was any intent to do so. This

should not be hard to believe since in the many years that I have known you, I have looked upon you as one of the family. Had I not treated you as such we would have had a confrontation a very long long time ago.

The incident that occurred in February of this year did not develop by design. It just happened. Before I go any further I would like to point out that I have differed vehemently many times with people I have loved and love, including my mother and father, my wife and each and every one of my children. At no time did my love waver, because of these differences.

Removing Andrea's masterpiece from the wall without discussing it, I admit, was wrong. But, this in no way should be interpreted that you are rejected and not accepted in the family. As a person I have a high esteem for your talents and social graces and I only hope that you will accept my explanation and if you feel there is need for further discussion, then let's do discuss it as father and son would, person to person.

I will be very pleased if you and Max would arrange to come to dinner in Hillcrest—soon.

Best regards,
Dad Desir

To which a week later Nick replied:

It's a hard thing to do, to resolve what has happened, but I appreciate your writing to me, and your apology.

What occurred in February is still very much with me, I am sorry to say. It seemed to me then a betrayal of what I thought of as an open, affectionate and respectful relationship. Your act displayed a kind of rigidity and cruelty that I was simply unprepared for. By seeking to destroy what was a beautiful and loving gesture by a beautiful and loving child, you betrayed more than our relationship, you betrayed fifteen years of family. Part of the pain of all this is that the large world seems intent on this same lesson of bigotry and intolerance. The large world, though, can be held at bay; you can retreat to loving friends and family for sustenance and self-respect. When, in that retreat, you are stung with the same venom as in the outside world, the wound is all the more devastating.

I don't know where we go from here. Self-respect is such a hard commodity to come by; I am in no hurry to risk mine again. I would like to think there is some path back to what was; I would like to think there is some good that can come out of this. But I don't know what it is.

Still, to acknowledge what has happened, instead of ignoring it, to deal with it, finally, cannot be a bad thing.

I appreciate your writing to me, and I hope you will take these words of mine as what they are, an honest attempt to communicate my feelings.

Yours,
Nick

They did not go to dinner in Hillcrest. Nick took the exchange of letters as the first step in an involved rapprochement, to be completed in several formal stages. John considered the matter nearly closed. As requested he had rehung the tapestry—not in the den but in the upper hall—and had now written, he thought, a generous letter of apology. Nick thought the letter did little more than restate the issues. It did not offer to make amends in any way. And he and Max wanted the tapestry back on the same wall from which it had been removed—with the oval silhouettes of the three older girls done by a man with scissors in Disneyland; with the pictures of the beach house and the *Mara*, with Marie's needlepoint, with all the familiar faces—and not hanging in a dark hallway no one ever used.

The lifesize drawing of the monument, so large, white and flat, seemed a little bizarre to begin with—a camel when you were expecting a horse—the artist's idea of their ideas. Robin and Max made the obvious changes, widening the flutes, pruning the exuberant incised flowers that bordered the apse, lowering this, raising that. Over the apse, which contained the urn, just D E S I R on the stone, with Marie's name and dates to be on a separate footstone. No one suggested they have coffee.

Mary Kay was angry over John's negative influence on her life. She said Jack was already overworked. She said how dare he assume Jack would take over for him while he discovered God—although he did and he had and Jack would. She could never have been so frank while Marie was alive. Without Marie the consequences of such a scene—John left before dinner—were greatly reduced. Everybody concerned thought, We've been through that, this is nothing; and pressed on. The next time they met, like Max and John after the fall of the House of Pancakes, it was as if nothing had happened.

Jack alternated between being timid at the prospect of running Mara Products, and confident he could do it. He said to Max, I have clients who run six companies. I'm forty-four; we run the world. Max said he thought Jack and John were inventing each other and that it had always been that way.

Mary Kay did not want, as Jack's wife, to inherit Marie's mantle. Robin and Penny, in any event, seemed to divide that between them. Robin assumed Marie's moral authority in everyone's eyes and Penny incorporated or, at least, let bloom an array of attitudes directly linked to her mother. They both also allowed themselves somehow to look more like her. Robin now occasionally wore lipstick, which Max had seldom seen her do since her marriage, and Penny suddenly revealed, through the simple act of applying a certain color nail polish, that she had her mother's hands.

John now had two months to arrrange his affairs. For this to be accomplished he needed Jack, principally to run the company. After a lifetime of competition between them, it was more than a business deal they were working out, especially to Jack. On the phone to Max he said, Why am I doing this? My kids never see me as it is. But he knew this was it, and thought that afterward, perhaps, things would be different between him and his father.

In January John would begin a trial period of six months at St Mark's; this to be followed by a year-long novitiate and the taking of his first vows, including poverty. After eighteen months he would begin three years of school in Toledo. Then he would be a monk, like a priest except he couldn't say Mass.

❧

Max had been trying for months to break it off with Clive, for reasons he did not completely understand. They saw each other every eight or ten days, sometimes less. Max said, You're wasting your time with me. I already have a lover.

You're what I want, Clive said. It was a wall that

continually gave way, no matter where he pressed. At times he was angry that Clive enjoyed the luxury of strong emotions while he teetered between boredom and lust. He waited for an excuse to burn the place down and it came in the form of an unintentional sexual mistake on Clive's part that caused Max considerable if momentary pain. This time he threw on his clothes and was out the door in a flash. The elevators would not arrive and rather than be caught in the hall he made a dizzying descent on the staircase, drilling downward as if deep into the ground. When Clive telephoned, Max said he didn't want to hear from him for a month and hung up. This brief exchange was repeated several times. A few days later the doorbell rang and within the seconds it took for Max to answer it, Clive disappeared, leaving behind a red envelope tied with white string. Inside were joints, two sticks of incense, a small box of chocolates and a card.

I will wait the rest of the time. I only want to say I'm sorry. This is for your head. For the rest of you, it's here when you want it.

Clive

It's here when you want it was a generous statement with a hook in it. It meant take it or leave it. When the month was up he allowed himself to be invited out. They met in the web of a sexual vibration, nearest to a swoon, in which Max perceived himself and Clive as hanging from each other's neck from a height, looking into each other's eyes from the calm center of their swirling nerves; and Max said, This is it. This is what we can give to each other. Afterward, whenever he made some move to bolt, or threatened Clive with his attachment to Nick, it did not appear that Clive completely believed him.

It must be something, he said, or you wouldn't

bother with me. You wouldn't keep coming around.

Why did he bother? He was not sure he understood the reasons, or would admit to all of them. It might begin with the fact that in retrospect he could chart his thirty-third and thirty-fourth years as the peak of his physical existence. Up to that point he had grown into himself as a matter of course. His sexuality, after a late and uncertain start, was nevertheless similar enough to that of his friends and acquaintances to show that, in this regard, he was something of an athlete, something of a free spirit. At thirty-five, toward the end of summer, he had awakened one morning to see his face as it would appear five years hence. This vision was gone by the time he splashed water on his face and brushed his teeth. At thirty-six and then thirty-seven, parts of the vision did not wash away. He now saw five years into his future every morning. He continually fought back an incipient softness in his muscles and flesh, like Capability Brown spotting weeds in some perfect garden. How dare they? He thought the difference lately was a flagging interest in this constant vigil.

His body had changed slowly and gradually from one thing into another in about five years, although you would have had to have photographic studies of both to perceive the subtle changes that had taken place. He was longer, thinner, as if he had been hoisted up an inch by the knobs of his collarbone. At the same time his shoulders had rolled forward slightly, ruining the drape of his chest. These disappointments, plus others, comprising a whole attitude of aging, troubled him even though no one noticed anything different or diminished about him. But if they did not see it, he did; and he thought that soon they would see it too.

Besides the agreeable convenience of his arrangement with Clive, he no longer enjoyed the pressures and risks of parading himself through bars and discos or up and down the hallways of bathhouses. The threat of disease was frightening, the free sexuality of unattached men a medical disaster. His desire for sex now lacked the simplicity, the unthinking force of his youth. It was accompanied by the worry that somehow, and rather as a matter of luck, if he struck out in some new direction it would not go well. Clive spared him that.

He had made some effort to explain the existing complications of his life. He wanted Clive to understand that when they were together it must all be different— simple, light, without thought or anxiety. Nothing mattered except the achievement of bliss. That his mother was dying, and then that she had died; that he hated working for a caterer, where everyone was in an earlier stage of his life but doing the same thing—preparing food and shoveling it down people's throats; that the enormous difference between the way he lived and the way his family lived weighed on him constantly; that his father was apparently going soft in the head over Jesus; that it felt as if he, Max, had lost not one parent but two; that the contortions of his father's grief found expression in oppressive ways—secrecy, abandonment and retreat. He gave Clive these headlines, reporting them with considerable bias. But he could see that Clive had only awe for the loss of large amounts of money at the gambling tables, and respect for a rush to Jesus. To Clive, Mr Desir's conflict was not obvious so much as pure. It was the measure of his grief. Family life was complicated. Max shouldn't take so much of it on himself.

Beyond that, Jesus Himself had recently been wed to Santa Barbara Africanna, in a ceremony that culminated in the addition of a picture of the Sacred Heart—Christ with a slight scratch—to the little altar in Clive's living room. The Black Madonna had needed a husband. This had occurred during the recent misunderstanding with Max. It was a double wedding; across the room, Freida had become Mrs St Anthony. Where else but to the flesh or to the saints could those in sorrow retreat?

What Max couldn't say to Clive or Nick was that sometimes, on the point of coming, the floor opened and the image of his mother flew up at him. Death, he thought. Not sexy, he thought. The image did not linger and he forgot it afterward. When it happened again he stopped and looked. A connection was to be made and he would examine the image and make it; then perhaps it wouldn't return. She was dead. She was wearing a wig and a ruffled collar like Elizabeth I. The image seemed actual, like a theatrical production. Her eyes were closed. They remained closed. She did not suddenly sit upright and leer. Then it all fell back through the floor.

Clive took him to see a Haitian woman in the West Nineties. They sat around a kitchen table—Clive, Max, the woman and her nephew. The woman spoke only patois. She poured whiskey on the floor. She gave Max a white candle to roll in his hands while he thought of the question, which anyway he was to keep to himself. She took up a few dozen playing cards, lighted a cigarette and blew the smoke between the cards. She lighted the candle, dripped wax on the table, stood the candle in the wax. She gave him the cards to cut, three times to the left with the left hand. Closed her eyes, which then rolled back under the lids. Slight tremors in the exposed, fruitlike upper arms. Opened her eyes, looked around, said Bon jour in a small high voice like a child's and shook everyone's hand.

She lay down the cards, first three, three more and three more.

I ' a quelque choix .   Deux hommes . . . Une bébé. The rest was lost.

The nephew translated. Geddé says there is nothing bad. He sees the man you are living with. You are bringing down his luck. The father. Your father is going somewhere?

Away, yes, Max confirmed.

He'll be gone two months, but he'll be back. Geddé is feeling sweet today. He likes you. He says *deux femmes*, two women protect you. He sees your spirit. You are a good spirit. Your luck is bad just now. You must take a good luck bath. You must think to yourself that things will get better. In the meantime, some delay. A woman in your family is going to have a baby.

Clive took him home and bathed him three times according to the woman's minute instructions, using a fresh bar of Ivory soap, starting with the hair and working downward. Max stood in the tub for this cleansing, presenting each section of his body in turn as Clive methodically, clinically scrubbed his way south; with, occasionally, an extra caress—the nurse in love—top to bottom, ending with ten little tugs on the toes, followed by a liberal dousing of Florida water and a sprinkling of fresh rose petals. He was not permitted to dry himself with a towel. In Haiti one was at this point supposed to walk naked along the beach to dry, preferably at sunset. Nor was he to bathe, shave, or have sex for three days. Clive put the soap, some of the petals and three pennies in a white plastic bag and tied it shut.

Drop this in the middle of an intersection on your way home, he said.

This seemed extreme. That's a fifty dollar fine, Max informed him.

No one will see you. The streets make a cross. Clive crossed his arms.

Max dropped the bag out the window of the car at Sixty-fourth and Park, as if in the transept of an enormous church, far enough away from any of his friends, he hoped, to spare them his wretched luck. Anyone who happened to see the bag and pick it up would find the three pennies and know immediately that they had in their hands a bag of genuine spiritual shit. If, out of greed, they still kept the pennies, it was their problem.

Nick was dubious but sympathetic, and unaware of the more ceremonial aspects of the ritual. He said Max smelled like a slaughterhouse. On the third day Max threw himself into the shower as if over Victoria Falls. A film of dirt had become an itchy crust all over his body. His hair had turned to cardboard, yet was looking no worse, he imagined, than his tattered spirit. He often thought his hair reflected the exact condition of his innermost feelings. He reminded himself that Geddé had said he must think that things would now get better.

❦

John, Robin and Max met one more time at National Monument and approved the lifesize drawing of the tombstone. The drawing was then mailed to a small quarry town in Vermont. Subsequently a block of white granite was cut and hewn to the specifications of the drawing, but then, through circumstances never made clear, the drawing was mislaid. It would be necessary for John and Max to fly to Vermont for the day, to fill in certain details all over again.

He dreaded the trip. Since the scene in the Pancake

House he had seen John only with others and briefly. Now they must spend a full day together.

John picked him up one morning at seven—precisely on time as was strictly expected by both of them—in John's current Cadillac, of a not completely pleasant green color. The enormous car, the ounce-of-gold ring Marie had given him, the watch, the fine suit, the hat slightly reduced in size like the vestigial remains of the forties—John wore all these things easily, even negligently, and today he was in every way the successful man recently widowered. He had come directly from early Mass at St Jude's and his eyes were red. They pleaded with Max as he got into the car; behave, they said. Don't give me any crap today. Let's just do this properly for your mother.

They drove to the airport, left the car in the lot, and had breakfast after checking in. A man behind the counter in the coffee shop was one of the most beautiful Max had ever seen. It was implausible that such a being had not conquered films, Seventh Avenue, or the Sultan of Oman, but was instead breaking eggs at La Guardia Marine. John did not notice. The man smiled back at Max. His was a body reserved for the transubstantiation of visiting angels, with the same perfect evenness, proportion and symmetry found in the beautiful face; a body the angel occupies for an hour, when it becomes necessary to come to Earth, to feel, and in which, in that hour, is found the peak of perfect health and well-being.

The coffee shop was nearly empty. Two businessmen sat in the corner over Danish and the day's campaign, one a short bald man explaining to the other the dazzling nuances of salesmanship that by nightfall would bring them to the attention of their superiors. While Max ate his breakfast John read the paper. The counterman had arranged the bacon on Max's plate in the shape of a question mark. He would have liked to ask someone for confirmation of this. He ate the question. He heard the short bald man say . . . Got to keep hammering at them, day in and day out. John looked up from his newspaper and raised his eyebrows. A few minutes later they boarded a small turboprop through its tail and settled into its narrow sprung seats.

It was in fact too noisy for conversation. John finished the newspaper and napped. Max gazed out the window. They flew low and into clear weather, presently over a section of wooded land slashed here and there with roads. A number of lakes slid by. A long white thread of highway, perfectly straight, cut through the trees for miles and miles and in the middle of nowhere transformed itself into a drab little dirt road. He had flown infrequently enough to be subject still to the transcendental qualities of the experience. Looking out of the plane he saw momentarily through the windows of past flights, particularly his first trip to Europe—enormously high, cold tundras of clouds rolled on for thousands of miles, lit by a shifting, giant sun; or the descent, rather like today, into the miniaturized simplicity of a totally convincing model railroad town, perhaps twenty feet across, which he remembered from his friend Scott's opulent playroom.

A Mr Reese met them at the tiny air terminal. He wore a wedding ring, was Max's age but older. John sat in the front seat, Max in the back. John began the interview as soon as Mr Reese inserted the key in the ignition. Assistant to Mr Dowd; two children; twenty-two miles; Carter was making a mess; less than four hundred thousand people in all of Vermont; a little town with three working quarries; word one about the lost drawing.

The same few winded villagers ran about, reappearing periodically to wave at them as they drove by. The scenery had been cunningly faked. Reese announced the exact moment of the appearance of Mount Blaze, which rolled ponderously onstage jiggling slightly. Did they ski? It was a comment on Mr Reese's respect for the sport and the mountain that an answer in the negative from both of them caused him to lose heart completely and be silent the rest of the way.

Mr Dowd deeply regretted the inconvenience. He was paying someone six dollars an hour to do nothing but look for the lost drawing. The stone, as they knew, had already been cut. It was the details they needed—the apse, the incised flowers, the flutes, the lettering. He said the stone was presently on the other side of town, ready for carving. They would see it after lunch. In the meantime he could show them the base, the urn, and something of the factory.

He brought them into a cavernous room, piled nearly to the dusty skylight with blocks of marble and granite, and gave them each a white surgical mask. The din of a high-speed saw cutting through a wide slab of granite prevented Mr Dowd from pointing out that over the past hundred years, eighty-five of their employees had died of lung cancer. Marble lung, the union was calling it. The air was saturated with white dust that caught the light and made it part of a suspension well on its way to becoming a gray, luminous talc. The huge blocks of stone, surrounded by smaller, odder shapes in different colors, were without shadows in the diffuse, nacreous light. Momentarily the power saw ran down and the sound of running water filled the air, punctuated by the delicate chink of a chisel. Mr Dowd showed them the urn—a graceful, egglike shape in white granite, eighteen inches high—and the base, rough-hewn, eight feet long, three feet wide; another sort of coffin, Max thought, touching it. His mother seemed already to be in these objects.

Later they drove to another factory on the other side of town. The monument lay on its back ready for carving. The first impression he had was that its shape was aerodynamic: a concave slab with tubular columns like pontoons on both sides. It seemed that properly powered it would fly. He touched the smooth, powdery surface and thought of Marie's hands. He glanced at his father, who was standing back, his head tilted to compensate for the foreshortening. To get farther away from it, Max climbed up on a high stool. His father held him by the legs.

His point of vision was now six or seven feet above the monument. It appeared to float, to hover near the ground, light, buoyant and sleek. Then he saw for the first time that his name had been stenciled in pencil on the huge stone—D E S I R. He was aware that all the animals in the forest were watching him. This object below, which had been translated from paper into granite so magically—from doodles to stone as if in sudden stop-time—was, in addition to being his mother's tombstone, his own. It was his, it was everybody's tombstone he was looking at, whether he used it now, later or never at all. He recognized it as something with which he was already familiar, not only from the lost drawing but from recognition of the stone itself—as it was, as it seemed always and already to have been; as it would be when all of them were dead and buried beneath it. He saw somehow that even in the drawing they had got parts of it wrong. The top arc of the apse was drawn too high, the funereal motif of dead and wilted blossoms among the surround of flowers, while thoughtful, seemed lugubrious and did not exist in memory.

These changes were made and compliments exchanged. John seemed immensely relieved. On the trip home a delay forced them to circle Manhattan, Brooklyn and Queens two and a half times. The sky was a clear, darkening indigo, just after sunset. At eight or ten thousand feet they dipped in a banked turn. Wheeling over the dazzling city, John said, The bridges look just like necklaces ... diamond necklaces. Which they did. And the banality of the observation did not detract from the effect. Everybody off the planet, Max thought. We're all going somewhere else, where everyone is like me.

In the terminal he looked for the man who had made him breakfast. They were going to meet in a hotel advertised on television. The directness with which they were going to have each other would astound even the jaded bellhop. While John was in the lavatory Max slipped into the coffee shop, his name and number written on a small piece of paper. But the man was gone.

XII

HE IS AWARE THAT, AT THE LEAST, HIS LIFE IS HALF OVER. HIS bones have begun to settle. In a few more years the whole skeleton will shift like an old house. His hair will have further thinned, his gums receded, his lids drooped. His nose will not be as straight, with gray in his beard and on his chest; with lines everywhere, folds, pallor, disappointments. People will no longer turn to look at him, will see nothing but themselves being seen. The game will be over, then long over, and then just a memory. He thinks, like Keats, that his life is a thing in water. The evidence of his existence disappears completely, immediately behind him.

A voice teacher lives below them. Through the open window he hears the beginning wail of "Summertime" over and over, different voices experiencing the same tortured giftlessness; or ghostly exercises, bright high notes, long falling scales, short emotional triplets that seem in ascending repetition like vocal renderings of the perfect clitoral orgasm.

In the back he hears other music. Huge, chrome and vellum, big-band drums tumble as if hurled down flights of stairs. A piano, a saxophone; high up and reed thin, a flute presents the ideal liked a calm bird.

Several dogs belonging to the local supers live in the interstices of adjacent apartment houses. Two here are related, as the supers of the adjoining buildings are related. The dogs face off, through a hurricane fence that divides their territories, and snarl and rasp themselves into a stupor, arousing other dogs in the brownstone gardens down the middle of the block; the wild sound of maddened wolves fighting over meat. At other times a graceful Irish setter directly under their window has the habit of a single-bark announcement of its presence at two-minute intervals. Nick has been around to the other street to talk to the doorman, to find out the owner's name. It is the super's wife, Mrs Capitalia. Max throws open the window. The morning light blinds him. Capitalia! he screams. Capitaalia! The setter looks up at him with a dumb red beauty. The face of another woman on a higher floor looks across, sees a naked man in a rage. The dog, not having made the connection, barks again. Max closes the window, switches the heavy curtains, falls back on the bed in the dark.

They live the kind of life they might have predicted and hoped for, but only in a general way. Financially and professionally, the effect is approximate. Nick has not moved beyond the level of a TV soap opera actor, and Max cannot integrate his talents and his needs. His fiction doesn't sell, or doesn't pay, and his job is demeaning. The apartment they have lived in for so long is prewar and large by modern standards, but compared to Hillcrest or his brother Jack's place, it is simple, small and somewhat shabby. It is filled with the trophies and detritus of the Rome and Florence establishments, long since dismantled or, in the case of Rome, suddenly lost, snatched away as if by a roaring flood. Each of the surviving pieces sags in some way, either with its own recollections, its original bohemian intent, or its genteel life service. Max and Nick have lost interest in anything but an extravagant and impossible overhaul. Nothing is moved. All is evolved. After years of attention to detail the place coasts comfortably—like an old yacht—on proven design triumphs, in a sea of benign neglect.

He is working three or four nights a week for the caterer, plus the odd afternoons, waiting tables, tending bar, assembling hors d'oeuvres; at bar mitzvahs, cocktails, vernissages, dinner parties, bank openings. He wears a white shirt and black bow tie, a black vest, black pants and shoes, over all of which is juxtaposed a long white apron—the classic sartorial statement of the servant. He prefers to work in the kitchen or pantry, where he is safe from discovery and can make the rent money in peace. Often he has looked out from the equivalent of the wings and spotted a friend or even a table of friends among the guests. Everything he does as a pantryman or waiter is a distortion of his old expectations of being rich and glamorous. He is present at the experience but on the wrong side of the canapés.

As a waiter serving the crowd, he feels only humiliation at each small theft from his tray, offended by the oblivious disdain of social democrats. He does not exist, is not perceived. In the kitchen he is in disguise. All of them are moonlighting, but all of them are at least ten years younger. Even having confessed in this instance to thirty-five, he is, at that, by far the oldest. He has heard one of them say lately, Forty! Do you know what that means?

They come through the door with empty, ravaged trays. Max has a row of assorted arrangements ready to go: butterfly shrimp and snow peas, scallops and avocado, minted chicken on endive leaves, riddles wrapped in deep-fried enigmas, each tray garnished with a mauve orchid on a bed of kale. They talk about themselves, about sex and drugs, their dreams and moods, apartments, the phases of the moon, the crowd and its swinish habits. One of them comes in with the news that a famous guest is under the table, out cold. Another says, Sure, Tallulah. Another says, Really, to himself quietly every time he comes through the door. They are all actors, young and hopeful, or beautifully groomed models, or artists somehow. Because of their dreams for themselves they see the present circumstance in theatrical terms. At the end, when the guests have gone, they roll up their sleeves and put the place back together, as though striking a set.

But to Max each engagement, each one-night stand at the Clear Meadow Country Club or the Guggenheim was a repellent act of subservience for which he summoned in himself a calm and cynical demeanor. On his first jobs he had brought with him the enthusiasm and concentration of a domestically, yes, a homosexually inclined teenager helping his mother; wanting the evening to go well in the same way he wanted his life to go well. Everyone who worked there was gay, and he thought it was because such people could be counted on to want to ingratiate themselves, and to do their jobs properly, that they had been hired—the job interview, if successful, resembled a seduction—or because the owner wanted to work with his own kind; wanted even, and perhaps nobly, to provide jobs for a particular kind of person—

someone handsome, who might know the difference between French and Russian service, who needed a job quickly and temporarily. It was an attitude that didn't last long. The owner smiled and said hello to them, joked with them, thanked them, but did not pay them well and assumed they should be grateful. He wouldn't, perhaps couldn't, treat them like the anomalies they all were—princes of the stage, of the word, the voice, the face. After a while they either settled into an attitude of resigned efficiency or they quit. Few lasted more than six months. Max was considered a regular. He saw the next move, which a career in catering would dictate to someone so inclined, but did not make it. He thought perhaps he was kept on, aside from his skill in the scullery, because of his car, in which he was able to transport himself and four waiters to small, lucrative jobs out of town.

Driving back to the city after one such assignment, Max saw a pair of eyes staring at him in the rearview mirror. He rearranged the logistics so that Rocco, sitting in the center of the back seat, was the last one to be dropped off. Rocco leaned back into the car, smiled, and asked if Max would like to come up.

The walls of Rocco's apartment were hung with crests and maps and pictures of European kings and queens. Plaster casts and statues, among them Pope Pius, Napoleon, a Roman matron—perhaps Livia Augusta, with lipstick added—stood here and there amid the lesser junk, bric-a-brac, books, scrolls; amid dusty, colorless funiture that included a handmade octagonal coffee table painted over with thirty or forty heraldic crests: Rocco's folks.

I can trace my family back to Venus, he said without the shadow of a smile.

Rocco was surrounded and obsessed by his history. He had delved into every corner of it. On the whole, because of his father, Italy was his principal point of reference; Italy and the church, a taproot to the juices of the world. Through his mother he had only slightly less serious backup claims elsewhere. He preceded Juan Carlos in his right to the Spanish throne, but admitted that three or four cousins preceded them both with better. Prince Charles was ancillary, the Queen a tangent. Rocco's potential was worldwide. Beyond a certain vertiginous point, he said, everyone was related to everyone else.

In Italy he was a Colonna and an Orsini, from which family according to papal decree there must always be five sitting cardinals. He was a Borghese, who controlled Napoleon. He was a Doria and so by immediate extension, a Pamphilj. He was of course a Savoy, an Altavilla, a Farnese and an Este of the thousand fountains; he was a Cangrande who were the Doges of Venice and wore the head of a dog as a hat, an example of which hung like a stuffed pet on the wall. He was even a Defilippo, like Max, the which fact had ignited Rocco's interest.

Showing his insouciance, Max is sprawled naked in a high-backed wood and velvet chair. On the floor in front of him, beneath the octagonal table of crests, is a street cobblestone. Max puts his foot out and rests it on the stone.

Do you know what that is? Rocco asks, more than willing to talk, passing the reefer. Max stifles a clever but inexpensive reply.

I will build a fortress on that rock, Rocco says calmly.

In the Pines or the Grove?

Rocco's face remains expressionless, but the pain in his eyes marks this latest failure to be taken seriously. They are *not* naked. They have not just fucked like deaf mutes. His eyes say, Here is a person who doesn't believe in the King of Italy. Boredom, rancor, *buona notte*.

He leaves, while Rocco is in the kitchen, taking a

piece of paper on which Rocco had written Max's family names: Defilippo, Desiderio, Leone. He is taking back his grandfather, his grandmother in the factory, his uncle, all of them.

Max once met a man in London who was a librarian at the British Museum. He took Max home and after they had made love, they discussed the differences in their lives. The Englishman, whose name was Arthur, said Max had lived an enviable existence, having been well fed, well educated and encouraged to travel, while he, Arthur, had had to struggle for what little he had and had never been anywhere but Wales. As for sex, he had always thought Americans were the best, but had never dreamed one could do all that.

Led by this to a point of illustration, Arthur told Max a story he had read recently in an old journal in the museum's collection. The journal was the work of a British colonel, John Braithewaite, who was later an aide-de-camp to Lord Gordon, and who had sailed in his youth with Darwin in 1831, on the first voyage of the *Beagle*. In this journal, which ran to fifty volumes, Braithewaite had recorded his service as a merchantman aboard the *Beagle*. He was nineteen.

In Buenos Aires, he saw a man whom he described in this way, imitating the slightly subjective style of the expedition:

> *A finely built caucasian, about thirty years of age, six feet tall, with gold hair, fair skin turned by the sun the color of clover honey, large bright blue eyes, blond mustaches, the hair worn long and loose. Came aboard with Darwin for sherry.*

From the way it goes on, Arthur said, you can tell Braithewaite fell in love with the visitor.

How can you tell that? Max said.

From between the lines, Arthur replied. One always has to read between the lines for the queer bits. He thought the blond man was the most beautiful specimen, of anything, that anyone had seen on the expedition—a perfectly formed golden god in the center of the dark wild, the first white man to go into the *Mato Grosso*.

Which is where? Max inquired.

The Amazon Basin, Arthur replied.

But the church sent missionaries into the Amazon a hundred years before the *Beagle*, Max corrected smoothly.

But no one had got into the *Mato Grosso* yet. And no one got into parts of it for another hundred years afterward. That was the point.

The blond man appeared one afternoon while specimens were being taken aboard, Arthur said. He stood on the dock looking over the *Beagle* and the goings-on. Darwin came out and invited him aboard to hear his story. The blond man was British. He said he had been shipwrecked off the Brazils; with one thing and another he had been some months in the interior and had seen a number of settlements. He said the natives there lived much as the Jivaro before the church arrived, but were more primitive. Throughout this time he had been mistaken for a river god, he believed, and had been escorted through the area on a kind of ceremonial tour, taking part in native rituals. When he thought the tour was ended, he had done his best to leave quickly and in the most godlike manner. The tolls for the journey out had been paid with gifts presented to him in the ceremonies. He had arrived in Buenos Aires with nothing. He now asked Darwin for passage to England, in exchange for which he would provide a detailed account of his experience in the jungle—a story, he said, much rarer than any of Darwin's collectibles. Regretfully Darwin refused, saying they would be another year charting the South American coast, after which the *Beagle* was bound for the Pacific.

The next day the blond man returned and asked to speak again to Darwin. He had decided that despite the refusal of passage, he wanted Darwin to know what had happened in the interior. He had spent the night writing it down. He held out a sheaf of papers; but before relinquishing them, he made Darwin promise not to destroy them if he found them offensive, which he would.

I am a scientist, Darwin said.

Exactly, said the blond man.

Darwin promised and accepted the pages. The next day the *Beagle* sailed, leaving the man behind. Darwin read the pages under way, and subsequently threw them overboard.

Max is writing in the afternoons, sleeping late after work. He is writing a story about Arthur's blond man, walking through the Amazon in 1832, traveling from tribe to tribe as a sexual deity. To Max the sensibility at the heart of the story is no less personal than a journal, although the man in the story does not look like himself, being blond, with a blond mustache and bright blue eyes.

THE TRIBE

I address this account to Mr Charles Darwin, Botanist aboard Her Majesty's Ship *Beagle*, Buenos Aires, 30 January, 1832.

I had brought myself deep into the Amazon jungle with an Indian guide hired in Manaus for his appearance. After some weeks on the river, using a series of shuttles and local pilots, we reached a point from where we went on alone by foot, stopping each late afternoon to choose a tree in which to make a nest, like apes, for the night. My clothes and few possessions had been abandoned; I wore only a leather thong and pouch for protection, and stout boots which I seldom removed.

One morning the guide ate something he shouldn't have—apparently fruit he had just picked; although from what happened subsequently, he may well have been poisoned, perhaps with a dart—for suddenly he fell dead at my feet. After sitting with him for some time, I covered him with banana leaves, a custom it is believed here that greatly increases one's chances of returning as an esteemed banana tree. Marking the trees occasionally to maintain a straight line, I continued in the direction we had been traveling—west, into the fathomless jungle, within the outer web of the river's vast basin.

I had not been walking long when I heard distant drums ahead, which then were swallowed up in a sudden downpour—a daily occurrence in the afternoon—that clattered on the jungle canopy like polite applause. When the rain ended a few minutes later, the drums were gone.

In the evening I did as the guide had done and selected a tree, gathering leaves and moss to make a nest. I lay in sudden darkness, in the auspices of the tree, in a space filled with sounds receding and receding. Hungry and exhausted, I fell into a deep sleep, into a dream from which I cannot say that I have ever properly awakened. I dream it still.

In the middle of the night the drums returned, in precise rhythmic repetition, first perceived in my dream but merging into reality, amalgamating with shouts and a sudden surge of sound, as twenty more drums were added and a chorus of voices began a chant of vowels out of order. I turned and saw firelight flickering through the leaves and branches. My tree was less than fifty feet from a clearing I had not seen the night before. At its center the tall scaffold of a bonfire roared like a furnace; thirty or forty men and women danced in a half-circle in front of the fire, their faces and naked bodies covered with white powder or chalk. Now and then a powdery mask peered up and out into the darkness in my direction.

Abruptly the drums broke loose into a rolling four-quarter rhythm that brought more shouts and a disruption of the half-circle. Certain of the men and women came dancing to the edge of the clearing, where the outlines of the trees and the undersides of leaves flickered like mercury against the blackness. A few young women stood at the edge of the clearing and bucked and swayed as if impaled on something coming out of the dark. The men strutted and preened and shook their genitals, licking their palms and stroking themselves, fucking an imaginary creature that stood before them in the shadows. As I raised up slightly, I saw the adjustment of their faces toward mine. No doubt the firelight was reflected off my skin. But they must also have known I was there, for suddenly I saw a pair of black eyes below me— not three feet away—and then a hand even closer, presenting a small cup of liquid.

I pulled back in fright and surprise, nearly falling out of the nest, yet the hand remained poised and unmoving, offering the cup. The drums went on, the imaginary fucking continued at the edge of the clearing. The hand held still, presenting the cup, the eyes stared up at me.

It is the god who must obey. I took the cup and drank. I was helped from the nest and into the clearing, coaxed and touched. I was drawn to the warmth and light of the fire. I felt responsible for the two or three inches of air enveloping my body, as a glow, an aura, a field of light. The drums became a new language of instant comprehension, invoking an involuntary response. Upon or within this response, as if riding the crest of a breaking wave, we glided above the treetops, close enough to see the roosting birds and cats, the serpent's yellow eyes, the clearing with the fire, myself and the others dancing and carrying on.

We danced, while the fire burned. Rhythmically, to the drums, everyone coupled. I saw faces behind the chalk; eyes, features, nipples, breasts, organs in flower. Because the god had come they could have it all, not the ritual but the event. Women screamed and bit themselves; men swooned. The god danced from one to the other of us. We fell from heights. I was among the last to fall asleep in the pile.

I awoke alone in the nest. The clearing was empty, the fire out and cold. I found food hanging in the trees on threads; fruit, cooked birds, a gourd of water. I rested through the day, regarding the blurred pictures that had been painted on my body, removing feathers from my hair. I stood out in the afternoon downpour and washed away the flecks of color and gold. It was as if days had passed.

The next night I heard the drums again. They beat steadily for a time, then ceased, coming again later from different directions throughout the night. At dawn I heard a single drum closer by. Following it for some hours I came to a river; and was about to cross and continue west when an empty canoe drifted slowly by on the current. In the bottom of the canoe were a paddle and a water-skin. Bits of green stone—jade, emeralds, or glass, I could not tell—and small boughs of white feathers littered the bottom.

I had come upon the canoe in a long bend in the river, which then again turned west. Toward evening, like the evening, the river expanded. I came to a break in the trees on one bank and saw two young men and a boy cleaning fish at the water's edge. The boy looked around and saw me but was too surprised or petrified to speak. Then the three of them jumped back and crouched. I glided up to them and stopped.

No one moved. I took some of the green stones from the canoe bottom and placed them on the bank between us. This astounded them. They looked closely at the stones and began to talk to each other in an excited low babble. I got out of the canoe and approached each of them, lifting their chins to make them look at my eyes. As they had never seen white skin, they had never seen blue eyes and were terrified. They began to shiver, the boy first and then sympathetically, the other two. I petted them and they were quiet. I touched the boy. The nipples were well developed but had never been used in this way. I bathed him and he me; with the other two we bathed each other. They were familiar with the rest and initiated it themselves.

Canoe and all, I was taken to their settlement, back a distance from the river. The three of them babbled excitedly, telling everyone what had happened, pointing to me and saying my name, which in this case required a knock of the tongue against the palate. Four or five old men came forward. They touched the back of my hand to their foreheads; they knocked their tongues and bowed their heads. I was shown into an empty hut in which a hammock hung from the supports, over a floor covered with banana leaves with the spines removed. I sat down cross-legged against the wall facing the doorway.

After a period of excitement outside, objects were handed through the doorway—small gourds filled with color and oil, larger ones of water. Two women entered and began to clean and oil my body and plait my hair. When I had been thus primed, a steady stream of people, one by one, was admitted to the hut. Each whispered something to the two women. These two would confer and then paint a picture on my body with their fingers, apparently corresponding to the description of what was wanted, or to a portion of the body if health was involved. I was soon covered with markings—stick figures, circles, diamonds, eyes-of-god. The pictures in the genital area had all run together, as had those over the heart, these two areas being most often touched upon in the requests. When everyone had come and gone the two women put a headdress on me of white palms and feathers, and led me out of the hut and down to the river. All the supplicants had gathered to watch as the pictures were washed off in the water. To them it was as if the skin itself were dissolved in the current, leaving behind a pure colorless soul.

Afterward I was led naked through the settlement to dry. The women fanned me with banana leaves, everyone laughing, the men playing long flutes and drums. Night had fallen by the time we returned to the hut. I was given fruit and a drink that tasted like fermented banana milk. I was left alone and slept. When I awoke I was given more of the drink, which kept me in a state of lassitude that was extremely comfortable. Time drifted pleasantly by. Lying in the hammock I was only vaguely aware of what went on about me through the doorway of the hut.

After two or three days of this, I awoke clear-headed and found the place entirely deserted, every hut empty, every fire cold, the implements gone. It was apparent they had moved on, and that from the hammock I had watched their preparations to leave for hours at a time. I felt a terrible sense of loss and separation; of rejection by the boy, guilt over a great wrong, remorse at having missed or failed at an opportunity that would never occur again, and fear at being left in the middle of the jungle with nothing. In addition, my head and body itched. I was filthy. I had not been out of the hut in days, although it was only now that this idea seemed strange.

I went to the river to bathe. Such was my discomfort that I ran the last few yards and dove into the water. When I came to the surface it had begun to rain, as it did every afternoon at about that time, but this rain was different and did not stop.

Suddenly, both banks were lined with people. Everyone danced into the shallows, splashing and beating the water, lifting their faces in the rain and calling out. My expected return to the water thrilled them. Couples bathed. The boy and I stood in the water up to our hips. He poured an oil on the top of my head that lathered into foam and coursed down my body into the river. Everyone was doing this. The river ran white, beaten down by the heavy rain like flour or linen cloth, with only the sound of water, of the rain, the splashing and laughter. I am the first to kiss here. They had until now nuzzled to show affection, and held hands. The boy tastes like a mild rum, the women of ginger.

We came out of the river and set off through the jungle. A path was cut where one was needed. The rain had settled into a dripping down from the clattering canopy. No one spoke or made noise. They followed behind in single file, away from the flooding river, deeper into the jungle.

I remained with them until the rains ended and the river went down. I lived and was treated as a man, but as one who had received the god and might receive him again. The boy and I bathed every day, which they consider a sign of attachment. When I left I was taken farther upriver, to the edge of their domain. The canoe had been painted and filled with gifts and talismans. Had it not been made clear that I must leave, I might have stayed with them, and dwelt there.

XIII

IN THE BEGINNING OF DECEMBER 1979, ON WHAT WOULD have been Marie Desir's seventieth birthday, a memorial was held to dedicate the finished monument. Similarity to the funeral seemed to be John's principal intention. Beyond the accidents of fate, in the rituals and patterns of his days and weeks, he dreaded change and took comfort in repetition.

Max and Nick came in the side door of St Jude's as Father Bill, again imported for the day, was entering from the wings. Max stopped at a side altar to light a votive candle for his mother, an isolated ritual that happened to overlap with his own beliefs. The top, right-hand flame in the rack was from his father. To the priests and sacristans of St Jude's this candle had come to be regarded as an eternal flame. Beside the Masses in Marie's name for the next two years, the substantial donations and daily collection baskets, John would, within the month, be re-nouncing all his worldly goods to enter a monastery. In the six months since the funeral, prior to which he had not set foot in the place, John had become St Jude's most interesting and generous parishioner.

Father Bill opened the book to choose a recipe.

I think we'll do the *coq au vin* today, he said and read it through to himself. He spread his arms wide, turning the palms out, and read from the Bible.

You start with a firm fresh chicken, cleaned and quartered.

Max, standing between Nick and Aunt Phoebe, tried to think that his mother was in the back of the nearly empty church, in one of the last pews. He allowed himself to turn and look twice. She was there until he turned.

Nothing about the Mass pertained to him; a little of it—the short silent parts—to her. His father studied the goings-on, slightly tilting his head like a bird. His silent weeping made Max feel detached.

Father Bill said, Lord, we ask Your blessing today on Your servant Marie Desir. From across the aisle a woman looked over at John and smiled fractionally and sadly. She took in the family. This would explain him as the new regular, and today's visiting priest. She and the six or seven other regulars, spaced across the church like cloves in a ham, watched Father Bill's technique, looking for subtle differences in emphasis, in pacing, the surprising deletions, the added nuance. With neat discretion the priest delivered his short meaningless homily from the altar, rather than slipping into the pulpit, an ornate wooden cube topped with a pointed cone that made it resemble an open beer stein; instead he stepped to one side to address the patchy congregation without a microphone.

And so it is we see that without much trouble and a little care we can produce a creditable *coq au vin*, combining the Lord's directions with the freshest ingredients of life, each at the proper time, in a moderate oven. . . .

Everyone took Communion, including the regulars who mingled in like obscure family friends. Afterward a short cortege of cars assembled while Father Bill changed his gown. On the highway they were scattered in different lanes in no particular order except that John's car remained in the lead. Just before entering the gates of the cemetery, Jack cut ahead of Max in his Mercedes, in a manner that caused Nick to snicker and Max to apply the brakes. In the end everyone's car door slammed more or less at the same time, with clipped percussive reports like a fusillade of pistol shots.

He had been present earlier in the week for the actual installation of the monument. Since then the gardeners from Hillcrest had resodded and landscaped the plot. The pristine gray stone, glowing at the edges like soap, was flanked by two conical evergreens, and surrounded by small trees and bushes. Circling the bright green sod, a line of flowering mums of various colors had been set in the ground that morning and would be dead from the cold by evening. This square of vivid color was set against an insipid winter background of receding mazelike hedges and graves, beneath a blank, cottony sky into which blackbirds disappeared like pebbles in milk. The plot stood out sharply, looking not completely real, as if transported that moment from another climate or season. At its vivid center the urn held anemones, white daisies, stephanotis and baby's breath—crisp, tiny dots of color put in only a moment before by a florist who lingered nearby out of respect. The weak winter sun cast shadows through the skeletal trees, like nets that flickered and fell from their faces and the face of the monument, and then returned, like reversed firelight. Max, Robin, John, Penny and Jack stood with Father Bill on the circle of fresh sod, trimmed and installed like carpet a few days earlier; Nick, Pat, Tom, Mary Kay and the nine grandchildren, Aunt Phoebe, Greta and her husband and their two grown children all stood along the side. Father Bill, the magenta piping of his scapular a thread of neon hanging from his neck, mentioned Marie's immortal soul. A few phrases later he referred to Purgatory in general terms, not as an insinuation but as a universal possibility. The soul was a thing, now in another place that was comfortable to it or not comfortable. In either case their prayers for it would be beneficial. Max was tempted, even conditioned, to pursue this idea. If he could think their prayers might help his mother to change rooms, even to change hotels, at the resort of Death, from something cramped and overheated, to the accommodations she must surely deserve—which he imagined as the big white romantic rooms in *Flying Down to Rio*—it obscured the question of whether her soul had made the transition in the first place. It obscured even the more basic question of the soul's existence. Where was he prepared to begin?

With his own soul. He felt sure he had one. His spirit; this lived inside him. It inhabited him. It knew more about him than he knew during the day. It knew everything in his dreams. It was all his functions, memory, imagination. It was fear, love, and all the emotions. It was the total of these faculties and more, which he himself could never have calculated. It was itself a place, a point from which everything within him was knowable, from which all was visible and clear; a point in the middle, perhaps in the pituitary, or the superchiasmatic nucleus of the hypothalamus, a point equidistant from one and all, including the dimensions. The part about immortality meant only that time had nothing to do with it, nor space, except to say that if a spirit lived within him, like the caretaker of a big empty house, and did not move about, but stayed somewhere in the attic, then what happened if the place burned down? What happened if the house was blown up in an instant? Could the spirit be caught by surprise? This perhaps was a ghost.

In the case of his uncle Dan the spirit had fled the burning house and then, through a miraculous technique, the flames had been extinguished and the house saved. The spirit had thus been fooled, tricked into leaving. Where was it now? Roosting perhaps in an apple tree outside Philadelphia, waiting in the intensive care unit of Temple University Hospital, or standing patiently beside Dan's body in a nursing home on Long Island.

And at this moment where but there with them, her family, should Marie's spirit be, if her spirit was? To see the new monument, to show it to Mrs Koenig down the line; where else but there with them?

❦

Penny did Christmas. No one wanted to have it in Hillcrest, not even John. Robin had done Thanksgiving, so it was Penny's turn. Everyone gave John items of monastic interest or utility; it was considered a difficult shopping assignment, the most difficult in years. What to give the man who has everything, but who is soon, in any case, going to give it all away? He received books, underwear and socks, sweaters against the mountain cold, a reading lamp, towels—the things you give to a student or convict. Gone it seemed were the days of solid gold rings and mink paw jackets. Christmas dinner was exactly as Marie would have prepared it. The logistics of serving such a complicated meal to twenty people, however, which she had done alone for forty years, now seemed staggering. Penny's table, being the old dining room table from Indian River, and therefore more than a replica, gave him something of a shock of recognition. They crowded around it in the same way and Max experienced a particular feeling—one he remembered having every time they had sat like this in the past—at this table, with the same cloth, food and flowers. It was the feeling that despite the crush, elbow to elbow, he felt an overpowering sense of someone missing. Before now he had thought this someone was himself. He still didn't feel completely present, but now it was for different reasons; and he thought the others must feel it too, one way or another, because of Marie. Only the table was the same, everything else was different.

The food once served was delicious, to everyone's great relief, because it meant something remained of Marie. Later they sang songs and Jack played the guitar, which he strummed like a ukulele. "Red Roses for a Blue Lady" had always been Marie's request in this situation, and Max hoped they would not sing it now; but they did and it seemed not to matter. John stayed in the room but with a pained expression on his face and not singing. "Five Foot Two, Eyes of Blue" constituted another difficult moment. Although Marie's eyes were hazel, this had always been a reference to her and was usually the signal for John to start dancing with her.

The impression that his father, in entering the monastery, had found a way to kill himself politely had been confirmed in Max's mind. Robin agreed but felt it all depended on what happened next—a tubful of spiritual blood in Marie's name, or a return within a few months, a well-considered leap back over the wall to family and self. She said John had confided to her that it would all depend on whether Marie went with him or not. He felt her presence at the cemetery, in Hillcrest, and during Mass at St Jude's. If she was with him at the monastery, he would stay; if she wasn't, he would not stay.

The week before John was to go upstate, right after the New Year, he called Max and invited him to lunch at a restaurant near the cemetery.

When they had settled into their chairs John said, Max, I couldn't go where I'm going without trying to square things between us. We've had our differences but I don't think it's anything a father and son can't work out.

I was expecting you to call, Max said.

Why was that? John asked.

Because of what you said to Mom before she died. Because you promised her you would do something about—our differences.

Yes, I did, he said. But even without that I would still want to straighten this out. I don't think I could have peace of mind up there with this between us.

For a moment neither of them said anything.

How are you making out? his father asked, when it was clear that it fell to him to start the conversation. Robin tells me you're still working for the caterer, and Nick is about to do a play.

That's right, Max said.

I also hear you have some pretty big outstanding bills.

I hear the same thing about you, Max said.

Well, that's different. That's business, John said. How much do you owe? he asked.

I live in a different world, Max said. I owe what I usually owe.

How much is that? John asked.

I don't want you to pay my bills, Dad, and Nick doesn't want you to either.

❧ ————————————————————————

Max, I can't sit in a monastery knowing my son is starving.

We're not starving.

Struggling then. You can't pay your bills and if you can there's nothing left over.

It was not my intention to punish you by being poor, Max said. It just turned out that way.

Well I turned out rich so why don't you let me help you?

Because I don't need or want your help. I'd rather do it on my own.

I helped you before, John said. Why not now?

Because of everything that's happened, why else?

But what really has happened? his father said. I removed the tapestry, for which I apologized, and then I put it back.

You put it back where no one will see it. It shows how ashamed of us, of me, you are.

Well Max, here we are, at this one point again. What is it you want me to do exactly?

He thought about it for a moment. He would have liked to say he didn't care what his father did, but couldn't.

I don't know, he said. I think I want you to be proud of me.

But I am.

I think we'd better talk about something else.

John said, I respect you for what you're doing. It's not your fault for being what you are.

How is it that you think you can get away with saying that to me? Max said quietly but bitterly.

I didn't mean it that way. I meant what has happened and the way it happened is not your fault.

You said, It's not my fault. Whose fault is it, yours?

Please Max, give it a chance. I'm trying to see it your way. I really am.

You can see it any cockeyed way you want.

Now that's wrong, John said like a referee. It's wrong to shut me out.

I'm not shutting you out. But I won't be a hypocrite just to make it easier for you. Besides, you're the one who's joining a monastery, not me. I'm not shutting you out. You're shutting everyone out.

John shook his head and looked down at his empty plate. Is that what you think? he asked.

Well what the hell else is it? Suddenly you want to be a monk? When I think of all the speeches you delivered about doing something practical with my life, and here you want to ditch everyone and everything. What is it but shutting everyone out? Do you think if you had died instead of Mom that she would become a nun and never see her family again?

His father looked at him as if he had been struck, which in a way apparently he had. The answer to the question, however, seemed obvious and hung in the air between them.

Another silence. Perhaps I'd better leave, Max said. This is not getting us anywhere. He saw his father had begun to cry.

Dad, I'm sorry, he said, and the two of them sat quietly for several minutes, until John collected himself.

Look, Max, he said finally, just let me pay your debts, so you can relax and I can relax and have some peace of mind up there. No salary or allowance or anything like that. Just the bills.

Even if I wanted to let you, I would have to ask Nick.

What's Nick got to do with it?

They're his debts too, Dad.

Well, ask him. But please, Max. You're letting your heart tell you what to do instead of your head. You shouldn't do that. I'm on your side. I don't want to get in your way. I want to help. You have to believe that. What's past is past.

Nick refused outright, as Max knew he would, but something had changed in Max. The edge of his attitude toward John had been dulled, and he found this difficult to reconcile with Nick's continued, ever justified, dislike. For the annihilated, nothing altered annihilation.

But Max who had felt the same, now felt differently. He saw his father as struggling to hold up against something more than symbolic removal. The center of his life was gone. Marie was dead, buried, eulogized, memorialized-in-stone, prayed for, revered. Everything to be done had been done. John's devotions took the form of policing the condition of the plot, with gardeners and masons, of changing the flowers in the urn each week, of going to Mass in her name each day. Little else to do. These moments in church were the only ones he could bear. They were tolerable. He wept freely, apparently in the acceptance by God of whatever remained of himself after Marie. He feared death, which was a thief. To pinpoint the idea in some physical manifestation, it began with the urn, which because of the weekly flowers became a symbol of continuation, of life. He saw it as a point of life within the stone. It was this point he pursued in prayer.

In a letter he sent to all of them he wrote:

I must admit that this is going to be on a trial basis for a period of a few months or so to determine whether I am suited for this way of life. Life without Mom is empty, meaningless and uninteresting. I know that I still have my children and grandchildren who I am sure love me as I love them and it would be gratifying to devote the rest of my life to them. But I have come to feel that by serving God I will be nearer to Mom. Since I miss her so much and can't stand to be without her, the thought of this nearness soothes me and gives me peace. In addition, the thought of serving my church and my God gives me a new meaning and a challenge in the waning years of my life.

Would Mom want me to do this? I think yes, she would approve. In my eyes Mom is a saint and she is doing what she can for all of us in heaven. And while I am here on earth, I will do what I can with my prayers.

I have spent my whole life storing up treasures and making myself rich. And I realize now that I have completely neglected to prepare myself spiritually for Death. I am accepting the invitation of Christ to walk faithfully in His footsteps to store up treasures in heaven which cannot be destroyed or stolen.

Christ said, Whoever lives and believes in Me will never die. The fear of death no longer prevails because the partaking of Christ's glorious resurrection supersedes. Jesus seems to have entered my life and has invited me to respond. I beg you, my children, to wish me well and give me your blessings, as I pray God bless you.

John went alone in his Cadillac to the monastery. The abbot had given him special dispensation to keep the car. The abbot, who kept bees, was also pleased to allow John time off each Sunday after Compline, to visit the cemetery—an hour's drive each way—and to return in time for Vespers. For the rest John lived precisely like the seventeen monks in residence, in a room like theirs, down a long stone corridor.

From the first he felt himself to be at a tremendous disadvantage. His problem, more than the mandatory spartan habits and hours, was what to do with his free time. The others had projects, scholarly and physical, like the abbot's bees. They all read and prayed when they were not sleeping or working. Even when they dined, one of the brothers read aloud from the Bible or Thomas Aquinas. Only breakfast was more or less normal, if taciturn. The abbot immediately put him in charge of the financial end of things. In a letter to Max he wrote:

> The Abbot wants me to make a study of all business transacted, and handle all monies received, etc. I feel flattered and glad to have the opportunity to do my thing. He won't be sorry. I'll make this monastery the richest in the country.
>
> If you could meet me on Sunday, Jan. 18th, I will be at the cemetery between 1:30 and 1:45 P.M. and as far as I know we will be alone. I hope you can make it. Max, I am very happy we got together recently and bridged the gap between us. I wish for our relationship to be even better than it was a few years ago. I'll be looking forward to seeing you for about an hour or so. Give my best to Nick.
>
> Very much love,
Dad

He found his father standing at the grave; after an inventory of the shrubs they returned to the same restaurant nearby. As they sat down John put a number of lists on the table, and Max saw his own name at the top of one of them. He knew his father would have liked to put a checkmark next to it and was restraining himself. They talked about the monastery.

It was very cold, the food was dull and starchy but plentiful. With donations, the sale of honey from the abbot's hives and Christmas trees, plus the revenues from retreats, the monastery did about a half million a year, John said. This did not require more than an hour or so of his time each day. He had nothing really to do with himself, and was not sustained, as the others were, by the endless reading and meditation. The lists were for Jack, who would be meeting him after Max to discuss the situation at the plant.

Are you enjoying it? Max asked.

Yes, very much. My health is good. We pray a great deal. If you don't like to think and read and have something to do . . .

Why don't you start a project? Max suggested.

Well, I've been thinking I should write a book. I should organize my thoughts and write about my experiences.

What's stopping you?

Where do you begin? his father said.

When John had been in for six weeks Jack did something about it. It had become obvious from their Sunday business talks that John was not happy, or did not feel he fit in; was in any case probably not going to stay beyond the trial period. A visiting retreat master from St Louis advised him to be patient and to give himself the full six months, but Jack could see that beyond a certain point this would be a waste of time. John was happy but not that happy. His lists were longer, the product of long hours of sitting in his cell imagining the outside world ever more avidly. For his birthday, which fell on the last

🌳 ─────────────────────────────

Sunday in February, Jack arrived with the entire family, with gifts, cards, flowers, a cake and candles. They sat in the restaurant around a huge circular table by the window. Penny announced she was going to have another baby. The following week John came out of the monastery and returned to Hillcrest to live.

The baby, if it was a girl, would of course be called Marie, after her grandmother.

IT BEGINS WITH THE SIGNATURE FOR MY NAME, SUCH AS IT IS known locally, a repeated cartouche for drum, followed by an invitation to attend. Whichever god is invoked comes through me. Depending on the moon, I am the flood, the harvest, the hunter's god—whichever is white in their imaginations. I play them all, like a visiting actor in the provinces, having only to go where I am called, presenting the grave attitude expected of me. I find food in my path at intervals and whenever I awake. I find costumes and fetishes. Even between distant settlements my position is known. I am tracked from one territory to another. If I keep to myself for weeks, it is known. I don't understand all of what they think me to be, or wish me to do for them. I make every effort to bless them and to show no fear. I trust their drugs; but no tribe would survive the killing of a god. I am punctual, or as punctual as possible at great distances by water or on foot. The natives are pleased to have this specific and immediate way of propitiation. All that cannot be explained makes me holy—my arrival, my nature, my skin, my gold hair, my eyes, my placid acceptance of all attentions and offerings.

✤ ───────────────────────────────